Road to Rome

A Medieval Fiction Journey across Europe and into the Soul

Marina Pacheco

Marina Pacheco

Sign up for Marina Pacheco's no-spam newsletter that only goes out when there is a new book or freebie available and get a whole load of freebies!

Details can be found at the end of this book.

CONTENTS

Chapter 1

Galen stumbled through the night, walking as fast as he could while trying not to hang too heavily on Alcuin's supporting arm. He didn't dare look back, firstly because it would slow them down, but more importantly, because he feared the city they'd just left would still loom large.

He'd been so relieved to escape and so surprised to have Hatim's help to get them away from his uncle the amir, that the first hour or so of their mad dash had been filled with astonishment and gratitude. Galen sent a prayer of thanks up to God for their liberation and, after that, several more pleading for support to keep up the pace and put sufficient distance between them and their erstwhile captors.

The night was only cool rather than cold. But they were wet from the cart filled with human waste they'd hidden in, and so the wind that funnelled through the valley from the heights of the Pyrenees chilled him more than it otherwise might. The track they were on, slightly above a gushing mountain stream, was also narrow and steep.

The path might keep to the contours of the mountain, but it was also heading ever upwards. It was covered in loose gravel that Galen slipped on, or else individual sharp stones that stabbed his too tender feet. Months of only walking on cool smooth marble had made him soft. Fortunately the sound of running water and the boom and chirp of nightlife obscured their clumsy footfalls and occasional pained curse.

Urgent as their escape was, and try as he might to ignore it, in the end the pain in his guts and pure exhaustion caused Galen's legs to give out and he crumpled to the ground with a grunt.

'Galen!' Alcuin tightened his grip on Galen's arm and tried to haul him back to his feet. 'I'm pushing you too hard, but we don't have much time to get away.'

Galen rolled onto his back, blinking up into a star-filled sky and said, between gasps for air, 'Give me a moment... I will go on in a little while.'

'Maybe I should carry you?' Alcuin said, his anxious face looming over Galen like a pale moon.

'I can walk. Just let me catch my breath. I don't want to die, and that was what Zayd al-Ifriqi intended for both of us.'

'I know, but he whipped you and you aren't accustomed to running for your life along rough paths and steep slopes.'

Galen blessed Alcuin for not being overly specific about his weakness.

'It's alright. Just give me a moment.'

'I probably need that too,' Alcuin said, giving up the fight. He flopped to the ground beside Galen, shifted the strap of the bag slung across his body to get it out of the way and lay on his back. 'It isn't like I've been doing much lately either.'

'Is the bag very heavy? Galen asked, tapping it.

It was made from good quality cloth and he could feel the lumps of food and the long edge of a book. 'You don't think it's all ruined by the excreta, do you?' Galen asked, suddenly struck by the worry of insufficient fuel to get them over the mountain range.

'It's alright, I've already checked. Hatim knew how we were getting out so he took precautions: everything inside is wrapped in wax cloth. It should be fine.'

'Thank God! Hatim seems to have thought of everything.'

'Ha,' Alcuin said noncommittally.

It made Galen feel guilty once again that, while he'd been living in luxury, Alcuin had been imprisoned and made to look after Bishop Sigmund who was being tortured to death.

'Was it very bad for you?'

It was the first time Galen could ask such a thing because it was the first time in months that the two of them were alone and could speak freely.

'Mostly it was just boring, being locked in a cell day after day, week after week, with nothing to do. Although it got better once I could paint. But the worst was not knowing what had happened to you, nor what was going to happen next.'

'It was the same for me, although I was less bored, for I was learning Arabic.'

'Did you learn much?'

'Enough to understand their speech and decipher their writing.'

'Will that be of any use?'

'They are an advanced people and very lettered. If we could get our hands on only a part of their hundreds of thousands of books, it would add greatly to our knowledge.'

'But is their knowledge worth having? Are they right or merely misguided?'

'I don't know. I have very little to compare it against, but what I read of their work sounded right. And their numbers... well, that could really make our lives easier.'

'You sound as though you admire them.'

'Maybe I do a little,' Galen said and then wondered whether it was acceptable to admire the Moors, or at least some of their culture.

'Well,' Alcuin said, 'I wouldn't feel too bad about it. We are bound to not be the first travellers to come upon the Moors' wisdom. Maybe others can tell us how much of it to believe and what to ignore.'

Alcuin turned his head in the dark to examine Galen, who tried to put a hasty lid on his thoughts. But he was too late.

'You look dubious. It's not the first time this has struck me. While your belief in God is unflinching, I have sometimes felt that your belief in the church elders and their wisdom is not as complete.'

'Do you think so?'

Galen kept his gaze fixed on the half moon and the ring of mountain peaks that surrounded him. They had only just started their escape and he feared what lay ahead almost as much as what they had just escaped.

'Sometimes you questioned the conclusions people drew about the saints, even if only to me,' Alcuin said. 'And you are ambivalent about the hierarchy.'

This was dangerous territory and Galen wasn't willing to venture into it, especially not while his nerves jangled over their escape. The prickly ground was also cold and it was probably that which caused him to shudder and push himself up onto his hands and knees.

'We should go on.'

Alcuin shoved himself onto his feet and took a strong grasp of Galen's arm to pull him the rest of the way up.

'Are you rested enough?'

'I'll do,' Galen said and, still not looking back, took a painful step onwards. 'Besides, the smell seems to lessen when we walk.'

Alcuin laughed, happy to be diverted by Galen's mild attempt at jocularity. The stink was another trial to be borne, and one Galen had not meant to complain about since there wasn't time to wash it off.

Every muscle in Alcuin's body ached as he stumbled forward, focused on getting one foot in front of the other, half dragging, half carrying Galen. He felt dizzy and weak and a roaring filled his ears.

He rounded a bend and staggered to a surprised stop. The roaring wasn't a result of exhaustion. Dead ahead was a waterfall. It dropped hundreds of feet down a sheer cliff into a circular pool. Water then gushed away into the stream that their narrow mountain track had been following.

'Have we stopped?' Galen muttered.

Alcuin worried that he might have grown feverish from overexertion. Then he realised that the top of the waterfall was lit by a silvery early morning sheen, which meant it was time for them to hide, thank God.

'I... I can go no further,' Galen said, and it felt like he was about to slip out of Alcuin's arms.

'You've done well to get this far,' Alcuin said, hanging onto Galen with both arms around his waist to keep him upright. 'There's just one thing the two of us need to do before we rest.'

'What's that?' Galen asked.

It looked like it took a superhuman effort for him to keep his eyes open.

'The stream up till now was too shallow to do more than wash our feet, but we can't continue like this, covered in excrement. Even in my exhausted state I can barely stand it. Not to mention that if they send anyone after us, they wouldn't even need dogs to track us down by scent.'

Galen looked about dully until his gaze fell upon the pool, and he gave a slight nod.

Alcuin tipped the contents of his bag carefully onto a tussock of dry grass, inspecting each item to ensure they were all clean. Then he turned back to the pool and Galen, who was swaying where he stood.

'It will be cold. Getting it over with quickly is best,' Alcuin said as he surged and stumbled with Galen into the depths. 'Ah, ah, ah!'

Alcuin's lungs felt frozen and incapable of drawing in anything sustaining.

'C...c...cold,' Galen whispered.

They were both accustomed to cold water, but this was something else.

'It must come straight from the snowy peaks,' Alcuin said as he rubbed Galen down. 'This frigid water can't be good for us, but we at least need to get the shit caked into our hair and clothes washed away.'

As quickly as he could, Alcuin hauled them back onto the gravel beach, still gasping and trembling. They were so cold Galen's lips and fingernails had turned blue.

'Alright, let's find somewhere to rest.'

Alcuin first squeezed the water out of Galen's robes, then his own, and finally the bag. He scooped up the three wax-cloth wrapped packages of books, medicines and food and put them back into the bag before he finally looked around in the brightening day.

They didn't have much time left to hide, so Alcuin supported Galen to the least steep of the slopes that surrounded them. It was still exceptionally steep. The valley dropped from lofty peaks into a v-shaped space with the river running down the centre. Thankfully, the slopes were wooded and rocky, with plenty of hiding places.

He had to act quickly since their disappearance from the palace must surely have been discovered by now and the soldiers would have been dispatched to recapture them. At least, that was what Hatim had warned them to expect. It was what had spurred Alcuin and Galen to keep going despite their exhaustion, and both were keeping a wary ear open for riders during their long dash.

At least, *he* still was. Galen sagged in Alcuin's arms, wheezing and as close to passing out as made no difference. Alcuin resisted heading towards the densest patch of woodland, or any obvious rock outcrops. If anything was going to be searched, it would be that. Instead, he dragged Galen up the slope to a moderate mound of scrub and rocks that would just hide them.

'You're limping.'

'I believe I have developed blisters,' Galen said.

'Well, I'll see what I can do for them in a moment.'

Alcuin manoeuvred Galen into a crack between two granite boulders and settled up against him. A scratchy gorse bush covered in yellow flowers obstructed his view of the path below and hid them from anyone who came down the track.

He could feel Galen shivering through their sopping robes and said, 'At least we know the strength of the sun here. You'll warm up as soon as the rays reach us.'

'I hope so,' Galen said, giving a wan attempt at a smile.

His pallor alarmed Alcuin.

'Are you alright? You haven't started to bleed, have you?'

'Miraculously, not.'

'Alright, then just rest.'

Alcuin lay head down so that he could peek at the path from beneath the bushes. At the moment, it was all quiet and birdsong filled the air. A trio of deer came to drink at the pool. Then a herd of mountain goats with astonishingly large curving horns appeared and started grazing the short grass by the water's edge where they were joined by a covey of plump partridges pecking about.

The goats pricked up their ears and all turned to face the path, which startled Alcuin out of his slide into dreams. The partridges burst into whirring flight and the goats scattered as a line of a dozen soldiers came riding into view, their eyes sweeping this way and that.

Alcuin held his breath and didn't even dare blink. Hatim was at the head of this band. He looked fierce and much more like a warrior in his armour. If he and Galen were spotted now, Hatim wouldn't be able to help them, not with all the witnesses. Alcuin lay as still as the dead and prayed that Galen would do the same.

The soldiers vanished around a curve of the mountain track and Alcuin breathed a sigh of relief but didn't dare move. He and Galen would have to stay where they were for the rest of the day, for they couldn't risk moving lest they be caught out in the open if, or, when Hatim and his men turned around and came back.

Alcuin glanced back at Galen, intending to reassure him. But Galen was curled up in his usual hunched posture, fast asleep, his face pale and lined. It had been a long time since Alcuin had watched over a sleeping Galen and he was sorry to see so little change in his friend. It seemed that the Moor, just like the king's leech and Brother Benesing before that, was unable to heal his friend.

Alcuin sighed and went back to watching the road. The sun had warmed him to a point where he was no longer shivering. His robes were also starting to dry, and now he noticed the result of his unaccustomed exertion.

He, too, had developed blisters, which he would say nothing about. His leg muscles were so tired they ached. No matter what position he chose, he got no relief. His back and right arm, especially, throbbed from carrying Galen and this was only their first day.

Still, despite everything, it was good to be free. God willing, they would continue to be so. Alcuin thanked God in several prayers throughout the day while he continued his watch.

Around dusk, Hatim and his men came riding back. They were going more slowly now and had the listless look of men sent on a pointless mission. They weren't even looking around anymore. Alcuin was relieved to see them go. He'd been worrying about how he and Galen could pass them come nightfall if they'd remained ahead of them.

'What was that?' Galen whispered.

'Hatim's just gone past, headed back to his uncle's city.'

'So he didn't get into trouble.'

'Doesn't look like it. In fact, he looked serene.'

'Good.' Galen looked about for a few moments, gathering the fact that it was growing dark. 'Have you slept at all?'

'I thought somebody should stay on guard, just in case.'

'Well, you'd better get some sleep now. I'll watch over you.'

Alcuin arched an eyebrow at Galen and examined his pale face. He looked determined. Despite a night without sleep and a very trying time before that, Alcuin wasn't actually sleepy. He suspected that was because he was still on high alert, ready to fight or flee at a moment's notice. But Galen was right that he should at least try to rest, for the road ahead would grow ever more arduous.

'Very well, thank you. You may as well have your supper whilst I sleep. I've divided our supplies into six meals each, which will hopefully last until we get into friendlier lands. With our distinctive robes, it would be too dangerous to go into a village asking for alms. We'd be far too easily remembered and reported on.'

Galen nodded. 'You are always looking out for me, Alcuin, but now you must sleep.'

Chapter 2

Galen sat as still as stone on the side of the mountain and watched the sun go down. He'd never seen peaks so high, nor such a deep valley and impressive waterfall. It was also fascinating to see how the shadows raced along the valley and shrouded everything in night whilst the tips of the mountains still flared in dazzling bright sunshine which lingered and stained the high snow in oranges and violets.

Galen began thinking of descriptions of these mountains to give his mother when he got home. She'd enjoy hearing about them. He caught his breath at that thought.

He was so far from home, and there were too many dangers ahead to take anything for granted. He was still deep in this melancholy thought when he realised it was now fully night and the stars and the moon rode high in the sky. It was time to wake Alcuin and get going again.

He dreaded this. It had been an agony walking all night. His muscles ached, his back was stiff and sore from the whipping, and the pain in his belly had got worse as the night wore on.

At first he'd hoped that the sharp insistent pain that he'd lived with for so long, and that Hatim had blunted to a dull, sometimes almost gone sensation, was a thing of the past. But a night rushing up the valley put paid to that optimism. Even a full day of rest had done little for the pain. Still, there was nothing he could do about it and they had to get away, so he wouldn't say anything to Alcuin.

Especially as Alcuin looked exhausted. He twitched restlessly and had a crease between his eyes, even in sleep. He snapped awake when Galen touched his shoulder, which made him suspect Alcuin had barely been asleep.

'Yes, alright, I'm awake. You can stop pawing me.'

Galen forced a cheerful grin and said, 'Tomorrow you can sleep first and we'll share keeping watch.'

Alcuin grunted noncommittally. Galen guessed Alcuin was keeping his peace, but also determined to make sure Galen was alright before he agreed to such a thing come nightfall. That determination was probably strengthened as Galen stood and realised he couldn't straighten fully. It hurt too much.

In fact, his body was pulled into the all-too-familiar curl he'd used at Yarmwick to keep the pain to a minimum. Alcuin stared thoughtfully at him, then set off at a slow pace, looking rather stiff and with a limp of his own.

'Keep your eyes peeled for a couple of decent sticks,' Alcuin said. 'On these steep slopes it will be useful for us both to have a staff.'

'That's a good idea.' Galen pushed himself to keep up with Alcuin. Despite the slow pace he'd set, it was still a stretch. 'And it should keep the wild beasts at bay as well.'

'Something else to worry about,' Alcuin murmured.

Galen looked up at his friend's strained face and felt instant remorse. If it wasn't for him, Alcuin would never have left Engla-lond and would never have had to endure everything they'd been through. He wished he had the power to spirit them both home, but no such miracle existed.

In all the teachings he'd sat through, and all the reading and writing he'd done on the lives of saints, he'd never heard of a saint who could achieve such a thing. Some had been blown along by the wind, some had managed impressive feats of endurance, but that was it. None of which he could achieve, although he prayed to God to make their journey as easy as possible.

It was the stories of his childhood and the more ancient belief in elves that kept occurring to him though. They told of men entering the fairy realm only to emerge in some unknown place or time. Galen shivered at that thought. They'd been away from home for long enough. It would plunge him into despair if he were to vanish and only return a hundred years hence.

'Are you alright?' Alcuin asked in response to Galen's shudder.

'I'm fine.' Galen was too embarrassed to reveal what he'd just been thinking. 'It's such a relief to finally be together again.'

'It is. I worried about you, since you hate being surrounded by strangers.'

'It was terrifying at first, but in the end I got to know Hatim and his cousins, and then it wasn't so uncomfortable. I was more worried about you and how you were being treated.'

'I knew you would be, and I felt your protective hand when they transferred me to a cell with daylight and gave me paints.'

That description of him surprised Galen. He'd never thought of himself as a person who might protect others, especially Alcuin.

'I merely asked Hatim to test your skill. It surprised me that he did.'

'Well, I was grateful all the same. It provided me with comfort and helped me hold on to my sanity in a place that was strange beyond understanding. I have never felt more out of place in my life.'

'True.' Galen was much struck by Alcuin's comment. 'Even once I got used to Hatim and the palace, I never felt like I belonged. Maybe that was another reason I was so desperate to flee.'

'Everything was wrong: the food, the buildings, the baths, the language, the art and, most importantly, the religion. We could never have fitted in there.'

'Until we landed up in Moorish captivity, I don't think I was aware of how differently people can live.'

Galen spotted a likely bare branch poking out like a ghostly finger from a thicket and pointed to it. Alcuin let go of Galen, who braced himself to provide his own support while Alcuin pulled the branch out. It was weathered and smooth at the top end, but still had bits of bark at the bottom, and a slight kink.

'What do you think?' Alcuin asked, banging it experimentally on the ground.

It was a bit short for him.

'It will do nicely for me,' Galen said. 'I'll keep an eye out for another. At least with the moon waxing and riding high, we are better able to see this evening.'

'A vast improvement indeed,' Alcuin said as he handed over the staff and took Galen's arm again.

Now that he had the staff, Galen leaned less heavily on Alcuin, which relieved him of some guilt.

'Belonging is a funny thing,' Alcuin said, returning to their conversation.

Galen was glad to do so. It cost some effort to speak, but it was wonderful to converse with Alcuin again after all this time, and it helped keep him awake too.

'In what way is it funny?'

'There are so many degrees of belonging. Like me, being part of a family, but not really belonging there. I felt more comfortable with the gang of boys in my monastery. We always felt like more of a family than I did to my blood relations.'

'And what of Yarmwick?'

'It was strange at first. It's a bigger place and, probably because of that, more regimented. And there were some trials when I first arrived. But it felt like home in the end.'

Galen nodded. Without his own presence in Yarmwick, Alcuin wouldn't have had the aforementioned trials.

'I know what you're thinking,' Alcuin said with a laugh. 'I felt you twitch. But Galen, I thank God every day that we became friends. You are closer now to me than any other brother, and we have shared many secrets. So don't regret the manner of our meeting.'

Galen was so touched by his words that emotion cut off his ability to speak and he just nodded. True companionship was the purest form of belonging. He'd seen it amongst warriors who fought through the toughest odds, and he saw it in the holy gatherings of monks. But, although he was thankful for it every day, he'd never really thought deeply about his and Alcuin's friendship.

'As long as we have each other,' Alcuin said cheerfully, 'we'll never be truly alone. Ah, that reminds me, you had a birthday while we were with the Moors.'

'I did,' Galen said, glad to be on a less emotional topic.

'So you're eighteen now, aren't you?'

Galen nodded, glad that the dark hid his suddenly warm face. His age made it sound like he was properly an adult now, but he was still so short and frail that he looked younger. He often felt helpless, like a child, even after all this time and everything he'd been through.

Chapter 3

Having a pair of sturdy sticks helped, Alcuin thought, as they trudged in a deepening daze, ever upwards. The river had turned into a narrow stream barely seen in the valley far below. The trees had thinned and now they were surrounded by grassland and, above that, towering rocky slopes so steep their sides remained bare, and so high they remained snow capped.

Alcuin shuddered and pulled his cloak tighter about him. The heat in Al-Andalus had been oppressive, but the mountain winds carried the taste of ice, and chilled him even when walking. For a moment, he almost wished he was back in Halab. But only for a moment.

Another gust of wind buffeted the two of them, leaving Alcuin feeling exposed. To make matters worse, the wind also carried the howl of wolves on the move. He prayed to God that they wouldn't run into those creatures, or the bears. They'd seen some deep scratch marks scoured high up a tree that had caused them to walk on rather than rest.

It felt like they walked far each night, but it was slow going because Galen simply couldn't walk any faster. They didn't stop though; not till dawn tinted the tops of the mountains with a ruddy glow. Then they lay down to eat and to sleep.

Alcuin's belly rumbled from lack of food. Jariya had given them what she could, but it wasn't much. As they had no idea when they'd reach safety, he drank his fill of water and tried not to think about all the walking ahead of them.

Galen never complained, and insisted on taking his turn to watch so that Alcuin could snatch a few hours of sleep.

'Are you sure?' Alcuin asked, yet again, although exhaustion robbed his voice of any forcefulness.

'I'm certain.'

'And you haven't started to bleed?'

'No,' Galen said with a tired smile. 'I think Hatim may have cured that after all.'

'Let's hope so. Be sure to wake me around midday so that you may also get some sleep.'

'I will.'

True to his word, as the sun stood at its highest point, Galen shook Alcuin awake. Alcuin might have argued and begged for more time, but one look at Galen's drawn face was enough to still his voice.

'Anything to report?'

'Nothing at all,' then Galen added, 'Actually, I looked in the bag of my books and discovered that Hatim gave me his book of mathematics.'

'Did he really?'

'He must have liked me more than he showed, to give me such a thing.'

'He must have liked you a whole lot more than that: he risked his neck to help us escape.'

Galen nodded.

'Hatim passed by again today.'

'Again, really?'

'Less than an hour ago. His uncle must be really upset that we got away. All the soldiers looked exhausted.'

'Do you think they'll come back again tomorrow?'

'I don't know. They came past later than yesterday and the day before that, and they came back sooner. I don't think they'll be willing to spend more than a day riding out looking for us. But we'd best remain alert.'

'I wish they'd just give up. But perhaps we're also approaching Christian lands, which will give us more protection. It looks like our path will start heading downhill soon.'

'I will be glad to be amongst our people again,' Galen said, then curled up and went to sleep.

Alcuin sat deep in the waving long grass, looking out across the mountains. They were so high up now that wisps of cloud drifted below them. A few of a peculiar creature Alcuin had never seen until he'd ventured into these mountains were grazing in a group on a ledge further down. They were bigger than a rabbit, and brown and chubby like a bear. Thankfully plant eaters though.

Alcuin was trying to fix their likeness in his memory, sketching an outline in the dust with a stick, when a high-pitched cry filled the air. A monstrous eagle dropped like a thunderbolt onto the little group of animals. It snatched one up, and, flapping laboriously, made off with its dinner into the snowy crags.

The whole thing happened within a heartbeat. Alcuin found himself shaken and more moved for the plight of the unfortunate beast than a man - who had himself been wondering whether the creatures were edible - should have felt.

And so the day of rest passed into a night of walking, and another day and another night. Galen and Alcuin stumbled along, too tired and hungry to even muster the energy for conversation. The fear of being captured gave them the spur to keep moving. That and the knowledge that there would be no food in this sparsely populated region even if obtained by theft. Not that either of them wanted to do that.

Alcuin was staggering along, barely noticing the path, vaguely aware that in this place of cliffs and crags, one misstep might send him plunging to his doom. He was thinking he should be more careful when Galen froze and his hand tightened around Alcuin's arm. Alcuin was about to ask what the matter was, fearing some sudden illness, when his eyes caught movement. Slipping down the side of the mountain like a shadow across the rocks, was a lion.

It reached the path, stopped and stretched, its claws extended and hooked into the earth. Then it yawned, revealing a pair of great fangs. Alcuin's grip tightened on his staff. His heart was beating too fast and too loud. Any second now the lion would spot them and attack.

The lion snorted, stretched again and looked about vaguely. Its golden eyes drifted over the monks and it lifted its head, sniffing the air. Then it growled and its hackles rose.

'God protect us!' Alcuin shouted and, holding it in both hands, waved his staff threateningly at the lion, shouting, 'Begone! Begone!'

'Begone!' Galen shouted, banging his staff against the side of the mountain. 'Get away you damned beast.'

The lion growled and slinked sideways towards them, baring its teeth that glistened in the moonlight.

'Come no closer,' Alcuin shouted and slammed his staff down on the ground in front of the lion who was just out of reach. He'd never been much of a hunter but he knew it would be fatal to turn his back and run. Not that either of them was in any condition to run.

'Together, Galen. Let's give one powerful roar together. One, two, three!' Alcuin shouted and the two of them bellowed an unintelligible noise that echoed away down the valley as they both banged their staves into the ground.

Alcuin hit his so hard it snapped in two and the broken piece flew into the air and bounced off the side of the lion. It gave a sharp, angry hiss and ran off straight down the mountain.

'Dear God, that was too close.' Alcuin was trembling from head to foot, and he wasn't the only one. 'What do we do now?'

'I don't know,' Galen said in a shaky voice, 'but I don't want to rest anywhere near that creature's home.'

'Definitely not, especially because the noise we made might attract people. Let's keep going. But keep your ears and eyes peeled for that lion or Hatim and his soldiers.'

The lion, thankfully, didn't make another appearance, but it made the two young men more alert, which was something to be thankful for, Alcuin supposed.

After another night of walking, they were back below the cloud line and the valley became more populated with hamlets of stone houses perched atop rocky outcrops and hills. It was obvious this was a place of frequent raids. Even the smallest hamlet was impregnable, especially to two tired monks.

Their steep-sided walls and shuttered gates were impossible to pass without being seen. Sometimes they saw people peeping at them through the cracks of doors or around shutters, but nobody approached them. Alcuin and Galen were uncertain whether the inhabitants were friends or foe and so hurried past as quickly as they could.

Chapter 4

Alcuin staggered to a halt and blinked, trying to get the world back into focus. It was nearly dawn and time to find somewhere to hide. There'd be no breakfast though. They'd run out of food.

Alcuin tightened his grip on Galen and muttered, 'Come on, man, just a few more steps and then you can rest.'

Galen nodded, but his head barely rose from resting on his chest as one leg plodded stiffly after the other. Alcuin turned towards a clump of bushes when a sound drifted over the chilly dawn air and stopped him in his tracks.

'Listen! Do you hear that?'

'Hear what?'

'Bells,' Alcuin said, and his tiredness dropped away. 'Definitely bells. Come on Galen, I think we're out of Moorish territory and back in the lands of Christ!'

They followed the path down and around a bend and there it was: a sturdy, walled monastery sitting atop a massive granite outcrop. The grounds below its solid walls were under cultivation, and a line of monks were working their way along the rows of vegetables.

'We've made it!' Alcuin said, tears starting to his eyes. 'We've made it, Galen.'

'Have we?' Galen said, looking around vaguely.

A large, heavyset monk looked up from his work, caught sight of the two monks on the road and called out to his brothers. They dropped their tools and surged up the path until they clustered around Alcuin and Galen, talking in a language which Alcuin didn't understand.

'Please, does anyone here speak Latin?'

'Of course,' said the big monk who had led the charge. 'We all do. Where have you come from?'

He was a fearsome fellow with a scar that ran from over his right eyebrow, across his nose and ended at his left jaw. He intimidated Alcuin, but at this point, he was just grateful to have reached relative safety. Alcuin laughed, exhaustion making him border on hysteria.

'Halab. We were captured by Moors and have been their prisoners for months.'

'And you escaped?'

'We did, but please, brothers, my companion is ill and needs to rest. Can I keep the explanations of what happened until after we've had a chance to recuperate?'

'Of course. You are welcome. We will provide you both with food and a bed. You look like you could use that. Just tell us for now that you weren't followed and that an attack isn't imminent.'

'As far as I am aware, we haven't been followed.'

Alcuin prayed God would understand why he said nothing of Hatim's daily search.

'Here, get on this cart,' one of the older monks said as he arrived at the rear of his fellows, huffing from the exertion of dragging this modest transportation. 'You look like you're at the end of your tether.'

'I can't tell you how grateful we both are.'

Alcuin helped Galen up onto the cart and then kept him upright by leaning against his body. The big, scarred monk took a hold of the cart's two wooden poles and hauled them up the path to the base of the rocky outcrop upon which the monastery was built.

'Just a little more walking, Galen,' Alcuin said as he took in the steps carved into the rock that were so steep an iron chain hung down beside it that the monks used, hauling themselves hand over hand to get up the rock face.

'I'll help from behind,' the scarred monk said.

Alcuin was relieved that none of the monks offered to take Galen off him. Neither of them would have liked that, even though Galen was struggling to stand. It took all of Alcuin's remaining strength to get up the rock face and through the sturdy oak door set into the monastery wall.

A curving solid base of the granite boulder formed the foundation the monastery was built upon. Another large boulder formed a back wall and poked part way into a simple courtyard. A small stone church abutted this boulder, which appeared to form its eastern wall. Against the opposite wall was a single, long, stone building. A roughly hewn stone statue of a saint stood in an alcove at the entrance to the building.

'We are the monastery of San Petrus,' the big, scarred monk said, leading Alcuin and Galen to the building.

Monks crowded about behind them, chattering and tutting sympathetically, but fortunately, none attempted to touch either of them. It spoke of a wariness around strangers, but it benefited them as Galen was anxious around people he didn't know. Although today he barely seemed to notice as they were shown into a simple dormitory with a double row of beds.

'I will fetch some food.'

The big monk disappeared through a door at the far end of the dormitory. Within seconds he was back with two pottery cups brimming with wine and two slices of a heavy, dark bread.

'Thank you,' Alcuin said, looking up at the circle of curious monks.

It appeared they had few visitors and therefore had no intention of leaving. Feeling a little shy of the attention, Alcuin held a cup of wine to Galen's lips. His face twitched, and he turned it away.

'Come on, Galen, drink it, then you can get all the sleep your body craves. I promise.'

It took a bit more coaxing to get Galen to finish his wine. Then Alcuin lowered Galen onto the bed and tucked a blanket around him. Alcuin wanted to tell him to be wary, or not sleep too long, but he didn't dare to with his audience. Truth be told, he was so tired he barely cared and he was in no condition to fight his way out. So he downed the wine that turned out to be spiced, ate the bread, answering he knew not what questions, then lay down and surrendered to his own exhaustion.

Galen slowly returned to consciousness. As had become his habit, he kept his eyes closed while he got a sense of his surroundings. He was lying on his side on a bed, a narrow one, wrapped in a coarse blanket. This was very different to Hatim's surgery.

In the distance he could hear the chatter of male voices, the metallic clink of tools and the crowing of a rooster along with a muted bleating of sheep. The room he was in was quiet save for the light snore coming from Alcuin. Galen had become used to the sound of his friend long ago, and found his snoring restful, rather than annoying.

This had to be the monastery, vaguely remembered as it was. The last few moments before he'd subsided into sleep had been a confusing blur of faces and the acrid taste of wine. Still, Galen remained cautious as he opened his eyes a crack.

He couldn't see much. There was the outline of Alcuin lying with his back to him, a whitewashed wall, and a small, deeply tanned, white-haired man with his hands resting palms together between his knees, watching Alcuin intently.

At this moment, Alcuin gave a snort and must have opened his eyes, as the old man said, 'Ah, my young friend is finally surfacing.'

Alcuin pushed himself upright and looked about, glancing at Galen who kept himself still and unresponsive. It was better for Alcuin to find out what was going on before Galen showed he was awake.

'What time is it?' Alcuin asked.

'You have just missed Prime, young man. But never fear; we will give you breakfast when you are ready.'

'Thank you, but... did you say Prime? How can that be? Surely I slept more than a couple of hours?'

The old man's face crinkled into a grin.

'You slept a day and a night. It is just past dawn now, but not of the day you arrived.'

'Oh... I was very tired, but I didn't realise I was that tired.'

'Uh huh, well, it looks like the two of you have walked quite a way. My name is Fra' Arnal, by the way. I am the leader of this little community.'

'I'm Alcuin and my companion is Brother Galen.'

'Unusual names, and your accent is unfamiliar to me.'

'We come from Engla-Lond,' Alcuin said, and Galen hoped he wouldn't be asked more. He still sounded tired and not up to thinking on his feet. 'Is it safe here?'

'From the Moors?' Fra' Arnal said. 'We keep ourselves relatively safe. We are a small monastery and number only twenty-three. But our lives are made precarious by being so near the border.'

'Why stay here then?'

It was a good question and one Galen wondered too, although he supposed nowhere was ever truly safe.

'To live by example to the people about here, and to our neighbours the Moors,' Fra' Arnal said. 'And to shine the light of truth into the darkest places.'

'I see. Have you heard what happened to Santiago de Compostela?'

It was another good question. By everything Galen and Alcuin knew of that holy city, it was far larger and surely better defended than this little monastery.

'No?' Fra' Arnal said, making his denial also a question.

'The Moors raided it. We were told they destroyed the place.'

'You were not there at the time?'

'No, why would we be?'

'I thought perhaps that was the direction you had come from.'

'Not us.'

'So, my son, will you tell me how you and your companion came to be here?'

'Of course,' Alcuin said, then sighed with pleasure to see a monk arrive with a tray of food.

Galen was glad to see it too. He worried Alcuin hadn't had enough to eat during their flight. His own condition made him less interested in food, but even he wondered whether he should open his eyes now too. But no, he'd wait, and discover a little more before the light of attention was shone on him.

'I am willing to tell all,' Alcuin said. 'But I felt so faint with hunger that I can't tell you how relieved I am to be allowed to eat, and something so blessedly familiar, pottage and bread. I hardly recognised any of the food the Moors gave us,' Alcuin said as he dipped the bread in the pottage and shoved it into his mouth.

'You were their captives, were you?'

'We were.'

'But you come from Engla-Lond?'

'We do.'

'You'd best start at the beginning,' Fra' Arnal said.

Galen's breath caught, and it took some effort to go back to the deep and even breath of sleep he'd be feigning. He hoped neither man noticed while he worried about what Alcuin would say.

'I'm an illuminator. Brother Galen is a scribe. We came as part of Bishop Sigburt's entourage to Rome.'

'His entourage? But there are only two of you.'

'We started off in a much bigger group, with the bishop and his personal guard. We meant to sail down some great river, I forget which, almost all the way to Rome. But a mighty storm arose,' Alcuin said, drastically abbreviating his story and cutting out anything which might arouse curiosity.

Galen opened his eyes now, but kept absolutely still while he listened, and Alcuin, glancing over at him, gave him a slight nod of acknowledgement. Fortunately, the Fra' didn't notice, or at least, made no sign that he did.

'The storm blew us off course and we were shipwrecked. By the worst misfortune, we landed on a beach where a raiding party of Moors was passing and they took the bishop, me and Brother Galen prisoner.'

'The Moors dislike holy men. But it is more usual for them to kill us than to take us prisoner.'

'I think their plan was to hold our bishop for ransom. He was travelling with a great treasure, a gift for the pope. I think the Moors believed they could get even more money out of him.'

'I see,' Fra' Arnal said, his eyebrows rising. 'They are a greedy lot. But you are no longer travelling with this bishop of yours, so what happened to him?'

'The Moors tortured him to death. They had just turned their thoughts to torturing me and Brother Galen when one of their number helped us to escape.'

'Why did he do that?'

'I am not entirely sure. Maybe he was a secret convert. We didn't have time to find out.'

'What was his name, this helpful Moor?'

'Hatim... I'm not sure about the rest.'

'Hatim Al-Qurtubi,' Galen whispered from his bed before he could stop himself.

Fra' Arnal looked past Alcuin and examined Galen with wide, surprised eyes. 'Hatim Al-Qurtubi? Are you sure?'

'Oh yes.'

Galen chided himself for having spoken up, for now he had more explaining to do.

'But he is the nephew of Zayd Al-Ifriqi and they are feared by all Christians,' Fra' Arnal said. 'They've raided many a monastery. How is it possible that Hatim Al-Qurtubi helped you?'

'He has a mind of his own, and, though I doubt he would ever become a Christian, he admires men of learning so he helped us, for we are makers of manuscripts. He would be in serious trouble with his uncle if word of his actions ever reached him.'

'You seem to have learned a lot about him,' Fra' Arnal said, his eyes narrowing.

'He made me teach him Englisc.'

That was at least part of the reason Hatim had kept Galen by his side.

'I see. Well I suppose that explains it.'

At this moment Galen noticed Alcuin's scrutiny, which always saw too much. Like how Galen was already tired by this brief chat.

'Please, Fra' Arnal, could we have some food for Brother Galen? Our journey was exhausting for him, more so because the Moors whipped him.'

'They did?'

'He has the wounds to prove it. So please, could I beg a bowl of your excellent pottage for him so I may feed him?'

'I will fetch it immediately,' Fra' Arnal said and hurried away.

Alcuin threw aside his blanket and dropped to his haunches by Galen's bed.

'How do you feel?'

'Better for having had a proper sleep.'

'And you will be even better after you've had some food. It's good, honest, simple food.'

Galen smiled and whispered guiltily, 'I was developing a taste for the ornate Moorish cooking.'

'For Heaven's sake, don't tell the monks that.'

'I won't.'

'Are you sure you're alright?'

'Yes, of course.'

'And you haven't started to bleed?'

'No, I'm fine.'

'That is good news indeed,' Alcuin whispered and then stopped as the Fra' returned, carrying food for Galen. 'I was wondering, Fra' Arnal, whether you might have an infirmarius who could look at Brother Galen's injuries.'

'I'm fine,' Galen said, not wishing to have a stranger look him over.

'We don't have an infirmarius, I'm afraid. We are a bit small for that. But we have several salves and healing drafts if you'd like to try them?'

'Thank you, just something for Galen's back, and for our feet. We've both rubbed them raw with all our walking.'

Chapter 5

Alcuin sat at the long oak table in the kitchen that doubled up as the dining table, happily chopping onions for dinner with Brother Carbo, the big, scarred monk. The man had taken Alcuin in hand and was acting as his guide. Not that there was much that needed explanation.

The monastery was the most basic he'd ever visited. Lean-to sheds were built inside the defensive wall. One for the tools, one for storing food, another for firewood, and in the middle, a workshop. A single long building with a dormitory, kitchen and the Fra's office ran along the south wall and on the north was the church that also doubled as the chapter house. All the interior walls were just whitewashed and the church's only ornament was a plain wooden cross.

The food, too, consisted only of what the monks could grow themselves. Even the wine - not Alcuin's favourite - was made from their own grapes. He'd already learned that the people of the nearest town had their own church, so the monastery was isolated, as they didn't even have contact with the outside world on Sundays.

Carbo had told Alcuin that the simplicity of their lives and the distancing from the locals was deliberate. It was an attempt to live the same simple life as Christ had done. Alcuin wondered whether this deliberate hardship was necessary. But that was something to be discussed in private with Galen. The devout men of this monastery had made their decisions by coming to live here.

Despite all this, Alcuin was astonished by how relieved he was to be back in a monastery. It might be small, and the monks spoke a strange language amongst themselves, but it was blessedly familiar. He hadn't even realised he missed the daily rituals of the church, or had valued anything other than the human companionship and being able to draw.

Having entered a monastery as a young child, it was all he'd ever known, and he'd never thought much about it. But here he happily joined in with daily life, attending all the offices and helping in the fields and the kitchen. It made him realise it was the entire way of life he valued.

Whilst he threw himself into everything with enthusiasm, Alcuin refused to allow Galen to get out of bed. Despite his protestations that he was fine, Alcuin wasn't convinced. Galen looked too pale and when he thought he wasn't observed, he'd pull himself into a ball and lie very still with his eyes closed. Alcuin feared that their flight through the mountains had harmed Galen's healing. Before he got him back on his feet, he wanted Galen to be fully rested.

In the meantime, he was content to do anything that was asked of him. It was a blessed relief after their months of travel and turmoil. He'd always thought he yearned for adventure, but when it had been handed to him, he hadn't liked it.

All he wanted now was to go home, but he feared his promise to Bishop Sigburt had to come first. He'd have to talk to Galen about that and possibly hide his own inclinations at the same time. It couldn't be helped.

Brother Carbo must have noticed him shaking his head and said in a bass rumble, 'You are deep in thought.'

'I'm mulling over how pleasant it would be to stay here for the rest of my life.'

The big monk grinned and handed him another onion to slice.

'You say that now, but you wouldn't be happy here for long. You have a greater destiny.'

'I'm more modest than you think. Give me a selection of paints and some parchment and I would cheerfully pass my days in drawing.'

'Aye, I believe that. I've seen you etching little patterns in the dust with your finger whenever you're free. But what of your friend?'

'Galen? Give him a pile of books and a quill and ink and you wouldn't hear from him in months,' Alcuin said with a laugh. 'Although... Galen seems to cope better with adventure than I thought he would. He's shy and sickly and didn't want to leave our abbey, never mind going to Rome, but...'

'But?' Carbo said, leaning forward to break the introspection Alcuin had fallen into.

'I think he's finding the things we've discovered, so far from his door, more interesting than he'd expected.'

'But why, if neither of you wanted to travel, are you out on this adventure?'

'I ask that of myself all the time.'

'But you are fit and healthy, while Brother Galen is not. And I know you tell us he was whipped. There is no denying that, but there is more.'

Alcuin looked at the big monk in surprise. He was a mountain of a man, someone any lord would be happy to have in his army, but he didn't come across as particularly bright. He spoke little and appeared to have to think long and hard before getting any pronouncement out, yet here he was, asking about Galen. Alcuin guessed they were all wondering.

He sliced his onion in half in a deliberate manner and said, 'Galen has ever been frail, but his mind and his fine hand make him an asset. That was why our bishop wanted him on this mission. And you know, there is no gainsaying a bishop.'

'So they made the little man suffer for the whim of a bishop?'

Alcuin looked up in surprise at Carbo. Was he actually speaking out against those who were more powerful?

Carbo saw the look, grinned and said, 'I've lived a hard life. My size made me useful and my lord used me to crush smaller, less powerful men. I thought it was wrong, which was why I came here.'

'Only to find that in the church, a bishop was pushing around someone smaller and weaker?'

'That's it,' Carbo said with a nod.

'Well, we can't always get away from it, but Galen has escaped to a point. He isn't pushed around by the warriors of my land now because he is a monk, so he has some respite.'

'It's still wrong.'

'I got it!' a cheerful red-faced monk said, breaking into the conversation by slapping the body of one of those small bear-like creatures onto the table between Alcuin and Carbo.

'It's about time,' Carbo said with an answering grin.

'What is this creature? I'd never seen them till we ventured into these mountains.'

'It's a marmot,' Carbo said. 'Brother Amis has been trying to catch that little beggar for weeks. They're great lovers of vegetables and have already made vast inroads into our root vegetables and our fruit. Hopefully getting one of them will scare the rest of away, for a time at least.'

'Are you going to eat it?' Alcuin said, running his fingers over the dense fur of the creature.

'Of course. It ate our food. It's only fair we get some compensation. You can make a soup from the bones and give it to your friend, Brother Galen. He looks like he needs something like that.'

'You are very kind,' Alcuin said.

Brother Carbo gave him a big grin and said, 'We are all brothers in Christ, after all. We look after each other.'

Chapter 6

'Alcuin, I want to get out of bed,' Galen said when he was brought his midday meal.

It felt like he'd already been in bed for days and he was sick of it, but he immediately regretted that he'd made his pronouncement so forceful.

Alcuin laughed and said, 'I've been bossing you mercilessly, haven't I? But if you'd been feeling well enough to resist, you would have, so I won't apologise for my overbearing manner. However, as you're so insistent, I'll help you outside. It's probably time we shaved your tonsure, anyway.'

'Thank you,' Galen said, for both the concession and the decision to cut his hair.

It made things feel like they were going back to normal. Which included Alcuin giving him a hand to get out of bed and an arm to lean on as they made for the door.

Galen smiled as he was led outside, feeling both grateful and apologetic.

'You know me so well.'

'I am beginning to.'

Galen arched an eyebrow in surprise.

'I am no mystery.'

'No, but your uncle told me that when you were a boy, you had a spark of life that drew people to you. I think I'm beginning to see it.'

'What?'

This wasn't something Galen had heard before.

'Sit and wait a moment. I'll fetch the razor,' Alcuin said as he pushed his friend gently onto the bench and hurried away.

Galen worried that this short walk had tired him and hoped that it was merely because of their enforced march. He'd assumed, after Hatim's treatment, that he'd be better off than he was now. Then again, he had made it this far, which was a surprise in itself.

While he waited, Galen took a proper look around the courtyard. It was empty, aside from a few chickens scratching about the cracks in the gigantic boulder floor. The light felt different here from the brightness of Halab. It wasn't as strong and there was a touch of autumn to the lengthening shadows and the coolness of the air.

Galen shivered in anticipation. He was glad he still had the cloak his father had given him. Hatim had returned it, along with his habit, which was the greatest gift the Moor could have given him.

'Here we go,' Alcuin said as he came back with a bowl of water, an old but sharp-looking razor and a strip of linen cloth.

'You ran off before explaining yourself,' Galen said as he dropped his head so Alcuin could reach his crown more easily.

He had his doubts about asking for more of an opinion on his personality, but his natural curiosity couldn't let him drop the subject, either. And now, while it was impossible to make eye contact, was a good time to ask.

Alcuin took firm hold of a tuft of hair and began cutting.

'You went through a great trial, Galen. It scarred you deeply. I don't think I realised how deeply till now. Bits of you, parts of your personality, are showing that I never even knew you had. I wouldn't even have known if your uncle hadn't mentioned it.'

'Oh!'

Galen was glad Alcuin couldn't see his face because it was so hot he was surely blushing. He'd always known the attack had shaken his never very great confidence, but perhaps now he was emerging from the shadow of that shattering event. It wasn't something he wanted to dwell on yet. Maybe he never would.

'I'll say no more,' Alcuin said as tufts of hair rained down. 'I just think it's a good sign, that's all.'

'Right,' Galen said and waited.

Even without being able to see his face, it felt like Alcuin had more to say.

'Since you're up now, we ought to talk about what we do next.'

'We go home.'

Galen cocked his head to check Alcuin's face. Something was definitely up.

'I don't know.'

Alcuin pushed Galen's head down again, sliced off another tuft of hair and flicked it away to join the thickening carpet around their feet that had attracted a curious chicken.

'Why not go home? Where else could we go?'

'To Rome.'

'Rome!'

Surprise suspended Galen's ability to think.

'Well, it is where we were headed originally,' Alcuin said.

'With the bishop, and soldiers, and money for travel. Now we have nothing.'

'Fra' Arnal tells me there are some monasteries and plenty of villages between here and Rome. We could make our way from one to the next till we reach that city.'

'But why, Alcuin? What would we do when we got there? Nobody would want to see the two of us.'

'I made a vow to Bishop Sigburt that I would go to Rome. That I'd tell the pope what happened to him and that... that I'd take you there, be you alive or dead.'

'Why?' Galen whispered, horrified by this revelation.

'Because he thought you were a saint. Because I've been thinking about it and I'm wondering myself, and surely you are wondering too. The only person who can tell us for certain, who can decide this once and for all, is the pope.'

Galen pushed Alcuin's hand back and looked up, examining his friend's serious face, and tried to imagine going to Rome. The long, long journey, the dangers on the path ahead, the ever-increasing distance from home and family, and the difficulty of getting back. He realised with a sick feeling that they had reached a crossroad.

'You'll go to Rome with or without me, won't you?'

'I should keep my word to the bishop. Now, I could take you home and then set off back to Rome, but I feel that as I am already on the path that I should go on. Besides, the millennium is nearly upon us. Who can say what will happen then? So I feel I should make all possible haste to Rome.'

'What of your promise to the bishop to take me?'

Galen was almost more shocked by that request than the rest. It seemed the bishop had truly believed in his status as a saint.

'The bishop never said *when* I should take you to Rome. I'm willing to wait your threescore years and ten. After you have lived a full life, writing to your heart's content, I can take your body to Rome.'

'If you ever get back from it this time,' Galen said and felt ashamed by how morose he was being.

'Come on, Galen! One thing I have known about you for a long time is that you are deeply curious. I thought you might wonder about Rome too. And maybe find it as interesting as Halab. Don't you want to see it with your own eyes? And don't you want some answers?!'

Alcuin pushed Galen's head back down with more force than usual and brushed away the loose hair with the linen towel, before dabbing a corner of the cloth in the bowl of water and rubbing at the shorter hair. Then he scraped the razor along Galen's scalp, removing the remaining stubble.

'It's so far,' Galen said.

'We're halfway there already.'

'How do you know?'

'Well... we already crossed the sea, and Fra' Arnal says if we head for the Mediterranean coast then we're bound to find a ship going to Rome. We could do it pretty quickly.'

'You'd be willing to get on a ship again?'

'If it gets me there quicker, and it's easier for you, then yes, I'd get back on a boat.'

'Oh.'

'You think on it. I've caught you by surprise. I've had days to consider this whilst you've only had this moment.'

'How could I get home without you, Alcuin?'

'Are you determined to go home?'

'I don't know.'

Galen felt bereft, struggling to understand what had happened. He'd just assumed that he and Alcuin would always agree, especially over something like this.

'Oh, my friend!' Alcuin put the razor down on the bench beside the bowl of water and took Galen's shoulder in a powerful grasp. 'I'm sorry. I'm forcing your hand, aren't I? I was so determined to go on to Rome I didn't really give you a choice. Knowing how difficult travel and dealing with strangers is for you. I know you can't make the journey on your own. If you wish it, I'll go back to Yarmwick with you.'

Galen nodded but now that Alcuin had floated the idea it troubled him.

Alcuin, though, gave a decisive nod.

'I'll ask Fra Arnal how we get home.'

'Do you really think I should go to Rome?' Galen said and instantly wished he could take back those words.

Why was he vacillating now, when Alcuin had already given in to him? Alcuin picked up the razor again and Galen meekly lowered his head so that he could resume shaving.

'I've spent the last few days thinking long and hard about this. I've come to many conclusions, one of them being that I don't enjoy travel very much.'

'So why go to Rome?'

'For that very reason. I have to do it once, so I'd rather get it over and done with now, then go home and never travel again.'

'Can you not just send a message about Bishop Sigburt from Lundenburh?'

'I wouldn't know for certain that the message had been delivered. For all we know the pope is in daily expectation of seeing his bishop and unless Penda got back to Lundenburh with news of our capture, people will think we are still on our way.'

'Or Penda could have got back and given the king the news and he's already written to the pope. We were the Moor's captives for enough time for a message to get to Rome.'

'But only we know Sigburt is dead.'

'True.'

'And none of that resolves your question.'

Keeping his head bowed to prevent getting nicked, Galen peered around to make sure there were no monks within hearing distance.

'Nothing happened when the Moors had us. And after all this time, surely people in the king's court will have forgotten. If we slip back to Yarmwick nobody need ever know and we can continue our quiet lives.'

'Do you really think Abbot Dyrewine won't have heard the tales by now? Or come to that, not ask us why we didn't go to Rome?'

'Oh dear,' Galen said as his eyes widened in dismay over that thought.

'Sleep on it. In the morning we will do exactly as you wish.'

'Why?' Galen said, struck by the unfairness of the situation.

'What do you mean, why?' Alcuin said, giving another pass of the damp cloth over Galen's skull. It felt cold now, a sign that his crown was bald once more.

'Why should we do exactly as I wish? Why shouldn't we do exactly as *you* wish?'

'Because I can make the journey to Rome on my own, dangerous as that may be. But you can't make the journey back to Engla-Lond on your own. To force you to do that would be to force you to your death. So, in effect, I'd be forcing you to come with me to Rome.'

'I could stay here.'

'No, you couldn't. They don't have a scriptorium. You'd be miserable without one.'

'I could stay at another monastery, somewhere halfway between home and Rome. You could stop there on your way back and pick me up. And if it was on a pilgrim road, you could find a group to travel with and be safer that way.'

'That is possible, I suppose.'

Galen nodded and looked up again to examine Alcuin's face properly. He couldn't bring himself to say it yet, but he was falling into line with Alcuin's opinion.

'You want me to go to Rome.'

'We've been on such a long journey together already. Do you realise we left Yarmwick in the summer a year and more ago?'

'Yes, I know.'

'And so many strange things have happened to us since then. I don't know what it would be like to not be travelling with you anymore. And really this... this question about being a saint, it won't go away. You should speak to somebody who knows about such matters.'

'I thought Bishop Sigburt might, but he knew as much as I did. I don't hold out much hope for anyone in Rome being any better.'

'Who can say? They may have any number of saints living in that city.'

Galen laughed and shook his head dismissively as his fingers reached up and ran over his now smooth scalp. Then he clenched his fists and looked Alcuin straight in the eye.

'Very well, let's go to Rome.'

'Are you sure? I mean you haven't thought about it.'

'I have, all the way through our conversation,' Galen said, and having made up his mind he could quell the last lingering doubts. 'You're right: if I go back home now those saint questions will still be there. Also, for all I know, they'll just turn me around and send me right back to Rome. I may as well return home with all the answers I can get.'

'Rome it is then,' Alcuin said with a relieved smile as he gathered up razor, cloth and bowl and headed back inside.

CHAPTER 7

Alcuin was on his way back from fetching a chisel Carbo had sent him to retrieve from another brother, minus the oaths of retribution Carbo had uttered for taking the tool in the first place, when he spotted Fra' Arnal making for the workshop. He looked rather furtive.

Although Alcuin had grown to like and trust the monks, his sense of self-preservation kicked in when he saw people sneaking around. So he kept to the shadows, slipped closer and put his eye to a knothole in the wooden planks that separated the workshop from the storeroom.

The old man stood for a moment, watching Carbo at work on a wooden bowl. Carbo glanced up, spotted him and bobbed a bow as he stepped away from the lathe.

'Is there anything I can do for you Fra'?'

'There may be, Bother Carbo. First, tell me... you've befriended Brother Alcuin. What do you make of him?'

An anxious tingle rippled over Alcuin. So the Fra' was worried about him, was he?

'He's a pleasant enough young man,' Carbo said. 'Nobility, but not workshy. He's willing to get his hands dirty on anything we ask him to do. Although by his account he's an illuminator and not used to some of the heavier work. His hands bear that out, being as how they're fine and pale and have no calluses, just like a noblewoman.'

'And what of the other one, Brother Galen?'

So these monks wondered about both of them, Alcuin thought. And, while it was never great to hear what others thought of you, it was essential, so he held his breath and kept listening.

'Well, Brother Alcuin tells me he's shy, and that certainly seems to be true. He hangs back and doesn't speak unless he's spoken to. Doesn't work at all either. Brother Alcuin won't let him. He seems to be afraid the younger one will do himself an injury. Which just makes Brother Galen embarrassed, although he doesn't object.'

'No, he does look very frail though and walks with a permanent stoop.'

'None too quickly, either. And Brother Alcuin was pretty well carrying him when they arrived.'

'So he was. He's very protective of young Galen.'

'Is something bothering you about them, Fra'?'

'Should there be?'

'I'm just wondering why you're asking about them.'

'Their story rings true, Carbo, but it's a strange one. They're an unusual pair on their own. But then there's this business with Hatim Al-Qurtubi. He's as ruthless as his uncle and no friend of ours. In fact, I'd say he holds Christians in contempt. Yet he helped Alcuin and Galen escape and I keep asking myself why. Why, why, why?'

'Maybe he had a change of heart.'

'Hatim Al-Qurtubi? Never!'

'So what do you think?'

'I don't know what to think. At first I thought Alcuin was the leader and Galen the follower. Then I started thinking perhaps Galen was the more senior one and Alcuin some sort of minder. But I've realised that each looks up to the other. I can see why Galen would look up to Alcuin, but I wonder what Alcuin sees in Galen.'

'He says he is clever.'

'And yet Alcuin is a clever young man himself. It makes no sense...' Arnal said and tapped his teeth meditatively.

'Does it matter? They'll be leaving soon. Brother Alcuin says they're heading for Rome and then you'll no longer have to worry about them.'

'That's where you're wrong, my big brother.'

'Why is that?' Carbo said, looking startled.

'Between you and me and these four walls, Carbo,' the Fra' said, looking around, 'I had a dream about Brother Galen last night.'

'You did? Heaven have mercy!' Carbo said and crossed himself. 'What did you see?'

'It was a strange dream.' Fra' Arnal settled himself on a stool, his eyes fixed on the middle distance. 'So very vivid. In it, I saw Galen walking alone across a great plain of fire and ash. He was walking very slowly, curled up, as he usually is. I could feel that he was in a great deal of pain.

'I knew, as one does in dreams, that Rome was Galen's destination. It seemed as though he'd been walking to Rome his whole life, and finally, he was nearly there. Then a wyvern appeared and lashed out at Galen with a great talon. Galen fell, the ash rising all about him, and he lay still, not moving. I got the strongest impression that he was dying.'

'Holy Mary, Mother of God,' Carbo murmured, his eyes wide in amazement.

Fra' Arnal smiled and said, 'Then Carbo... then God spoke to me. He said, in a voice of great power and majesty, "Do not suffer my servant, Galen, to die, Arnal!"'

This revelation was so surprising that Alcuin jerked back in fright, bumped against a sickle and made a hasty grab at it to prevent it from falling. Then, still clinging to the implement, he hastily put his eye back to the hole.

'God spoke to you!' Carbo breathed. 'What a wondrous thing!'

'It was terrifying. Not something I've experienced before, nor anything I wish to repeat.'

'What will you do?'

'To protect Brother Galen?'

'It is your sacred duty, after all.'

'Perhaps the same duty as the one which prompted Hatim Al-Qurtubi to act the way he did, hmm?'

'It must be.'

'Perhaps. But that is a mystery I won't try to solve. I will only work on the one given directly to me. I have considered the problem, and I have come to a decision. You must accompany Alcuin and Galen to Rome.'

Carbo's eyes nearly sprang from their sockets.

'Me, Fra'? But what can I do?'

'You were a soldier and you still have an intimidating build. You will frighten away any bandits who might lay their hands on Brother Galen. You also know the route to Rome, so you will be their protector and their guide.'

'If they will have me, Fra'.'

'They will, for we won't tell them why you are going. We'll tell them you are taking a supply of our oil to Rome to be blessed so that we may use it as unguents for the sick and dying. It is something we need, anyway.'

'I will do as you wish, Fra'.'

'As I knew you would, Carbo. You are a good and faithful servant of God.'

Alcuin watched the Fra' slip out of the workshop and back to his office. Then he realised he'd stopped breathing and inhaled. A prophetical dream? About Galen? He'd seen some extraordinary things happen around his friend, including the way his father had been stopped in his tracks and the lightning bolt that sank the Viking ship, but this new revelation still shook him.

Chapter 8

Galen sat on his bed in the empty dormitory and sighed to the depth of his soul. Telling Alcuin that he was fine with going to Rome was one thing, but as his strength improved, Galen found himself overwhelmed by the enormity of what lay ahead.

He'd been upset and afraid when Bishop Sigburt ordered him on the trip in Lundenburh, but he'd had less time to consider and no say in whether or not he went. This time was different. Now, as he gazed at the empty page where he was trying to list what they needed for such a journey, his mind was a blank.

Not that they had much: just the clothes they had on, the small supply of medicines Hatim had given him and his three books. Alcuin had assured him that the monastery would provide them with a supply of food to get them going. He thought there would be sufficient churches, monasteries and people willing to provide alms on their route, that the two of them wouldn't need to worry about starving to death.

'Either way,' Alcuin had said, 'we should set off soon. It's September already and I hear the winter around here is harsh. It would be better to leave while it's still good for travelling and head down to warmer regions.'

Galen agreed. He had no wish to linger in this little monastery, for, much to his surprise, it was boring. The only thing diverting enough to provide a distraction was Alcuin's inexplicable behaviour. He seemed disconcerted and jumpy, but he wouldn't be drawn.

He also kept staring at Galen and looking away when he was noticed. Time would eventually explain that one, Galen was certain. Alcuin seldom kept secrets from him for long.

Three days later, as they were about to head off, Alcuin had still said nothing, which was more puzzling. They had filled their sack with food and drink, and Alcuin was giving it an experimental heft.

'It's not too heavy,' he said cheerfully.

He pulled the strap over his head so that it crossed his body. Then he spent some time adjusting it.

'Are you sure you can carry it all? I'm more than capable of taking a share of the load.'

'You stick with your books,' Alcuin said and looked around.

The dormitory was empty, as usual. The monks had been working from dawn to dusk to get all the crops in before the winter. It struck Galen that Alcuin was waiting for something. As they had everything, Galen couldn't work out what was still needed.

'We have our staves as well. They'll be helpful,' Galen said.

'And you're sure you're feeling up to this?'

'I feel much better than at any point along our journey,' Galen said, repeating what was turning into an hourly mantra.

'Okay then,' Alcuin said, looking around once more. 'I suppose this is it.'

Galen took his staff and handed the other to Alcuin. Then he looked over the room one last time, making sure he was leaving nothing behind.

As they stepped out into the courtyard, Galen was surprised to find Fra' Arnal and the big Brother Carbo waiting for them.

He was more alarmed that Carbo was similarly laden, with a full sack slung across his body and a staff that dwarfed both of theirs, gripped in one massive hand. Alcuin might say that Brother Carbo was harmless, but he frightened Galen.

'So you are all set, are you?' Fra' Arnal said, beaming at them.

'That we are,' Alcuin said. 'Thanks, once again, for your hospitality and all the supplies and money you have given us, Fra' Arnal. You have been more than generous.'

'Nonsense, my boy,' Arnal said as he blessed them both with a sign of the cross. 'I just pray you have a safe and uneventful journey.'

'So do we,' Alcuin said with a crack of laughter. 'It would make a pleasant change for us.'

'As you may notice, I've asked Brother Carbo to go with you,' Fra' Arnal said.

The way he said it felt odd to Galen, as was the fact that he was springing this companion on them at the last minute, although Alcuin didn't even seem surprised.

'Will… will we need him?' Galen asked, because nobody else was saying anything. 'Don't you need everybody's help to get the crops in?'

'We will manage without Carbo for a while,' Fra' Arnal said, but his smile faded and his face grew grave. 'These are dangerous times. The end of the year approaches, and then we'll only be a year away from the millennium. You may think we are cut off from the world in our little monastery, but news still reaches us.

'The approaching millennium is having a profound effect on the hearts and minds of the people. Entire villages are selling off their worldly goods and heading towards Rome or Jerusalem. Cults of every description have sprung up like mushrooms overnight. And dubious characters are proclaiming themselves to be prophets or messiahs, garnering large followings. Many of these groups have turned violent, taking whatever they want and wreaking havoc wherever they appear.

'I would therefore feel happier if you have Brother Carbo as your protector and guide. He has been to Rome before, so knows the way. Aside from that, he is carrying a supply of our medicines that I have charged him to have blessed in Rome. It's something I've been meaning to do for a long time.'

'I see,' Galen said, glancing up at Alcuin.

He just smiled and said, 'We'll be glad to have you, Brother Carbo. The more the merrier.'

In fairness, Galen couldn't say much against having the big monk join them, but Alcuin seemed a little too willing. Perhaps Fra' Arnal's warning of ravening hordes had convinced him. Galen had to put aside his fears and accept the big man. He should have been grateful too. Travel had its perils and a bigger group was safer.

CHAPTER 9

As Alcuin expected, Carbo set too fast a pace, waving a cheery farewell to his fellow monks, who were picking grapes, swinging his arms and looking about himself. Alcuin wasn't willing to let Galen even attempt to keep up. Not that Galen was trying, which was unusual for him. Usually, he didn't like to hold people back.

At least he could walk on his own nowadays. When they'd set off from the Abbey of Yarmwick, they'd travelled most of the way by cart, and even so, Alcuin had provided his arm to support Galen the rest of the time. Now Galen was clinging to his staff, his gaze fixed on the ground in intense concentration, but setting his own pace. It seemed Galen didn't want Carbo's company.

If he'd joined their party for Fra' Arnal's just now stated aims, Alcuin might have left him to set his own pace, and not been worried if they landed up going their separate ways. But the Fra's dream haunted Alcuin. It made him wonder whether he was doing the right thing by taking Galen to Rome.

If his life was in danger, surely it would be better to take him home. But then again, the dream had also said that Galen had spent his whole life on this road, which seemed to imply that he had to go on.

This constant vacillation between pressing on or taking the more prudent path had kept Alcuin awake at night. He wished he could talk about it, but he couldn't broach the subject with

Galen. His friend had enough on his plate. Alcuin didn't want to add to his questions and doubts with a dream that may or may not have been significant and sent by God.

So, having Carbo was essential and when he got too far ahead, apparently oblivious to his charges, Alcuin stuck two fingers in his mouth and gave a shrill whistle that made Galen jump.

'What are you doing?' Galen murmured.

'Just letting Carbo know he's getting too far ahead,' Alcuin said, relieved that Carbo turned back to see what was up.

'Do you want to walk with him?'

'He's bound to be a better fighter than either of us, and intimidating enough to keep most bandits from even making the attempt. Besides, he actually knows the route to Rome. If nothing else, that is invaluable.'

Carbo, in the meantime, had settled on a fallen log and waited until Alcuin and Galen drew level before standing up again.

'Sorry, I shouldn't have gone so fast. Are you alright, Brother Galen? You look pale.'

Galen grimaced at him and Alcuin said, 'Brother Carbo, I'm afraid we are rather slow travellers.' For form's sake, and to hide what he knew, he added, 'We don't want to hold you back, so if you wish to forge ahead and leave us to our own devices, we'll understand.'

'What, leave the two of you alone on this road with only the faintest idea of how to get to Rome and with robbers around every corner?' Carbo said, and he sounded genuinely shocked.

'The thing is,' Alcuin said, casting a look at Galen, 'we can't go any faster.'

'Then I'll slow down. I'm in no hurry. And if Brother Galen likes, I can give him a ride.'

'No!' Galen said and backed away, his eyes wide with fear.

'Did I do something to offend you, Brother Galen?' Carbo said.

'You... you're just very big,' Galen said and took a further step back.

Carbo scratched his head in bemusement. He clearly couldn't understand why Galen didn't like him. Alcuin was beginning to understand though. Galen's comment about Carbo's size made a piece fall into place. For a moment, looking up at the big man, he'd realised that Carbo's build was very similar to Septimus's.

'Where are we headed, Brother Carbo?' Alcuin asked, to change the subject.

'We'll head east. That way we'll get into the foothills, which will make it faster to get to the sea, and it brings us closer to towns and monasteries too.'

'This land seems to be very sparsely populated.'

Alcuin had decided that the best way to get Galen distracted, and hopefully used to Carbo, was if they talked. Since Galen was never likely to initiate a conversation, and Carbo was of a stolid disposition, it was up to him to do the work.

'Aye, it's one of the reasons I chose it.'

'So you're not from around here?'

'My family are from further south, but I didn't spend much time with them. I was always a big lad and I caught the eye of a local lord who conscripted me into his army.'

'That must have been hard for you.'

Carbo shrugged in a way that implied it was the way of the world.

'It benefited my family, for they had one less mouth to feed and I had a small sum of money I could share with them.'

'I see,' Alcuin said, noting that Galen's natural curiosity meant he was listening more closely than most people might. 'So how did you manage to leave your lord's service?'

'I got injured,' Carbo said, tapping the scar that marred his face. 'I lay sick and fever-addled for a few days in the fields where the rest were fighting. When I came to my senses I had time to think and to realise how close I had come to death and how unprepared my soul was. I feared that if I continued my current life I would land up going straight to hell.'

'So?'

'I knew my master wouldn't easily let me go, so, may God forgive me,' Carbo said, crossing himself, 'I pretended that the blow to my head had addled my brain. I drooled and acted the fool. I wandered about aimlessly and pretended I no longer knew what to do with a sword.'

'That was cunning.'

'It was such a good performance that when the army moved on I sat down on a boulder in the middle of the camp, grinning and mumbling, and they just left me there. Thankfully, one of my friends put a loaf of bread in my lap as he departed, but I'm sure they all believed I wouldn't last long.'

It was a more cunning method than Alcuin had expected. But it had the advantage of being entirely lawful. Carbo hadn't run away, he'd been abandoned, so his lord couldn't execute him for desertion.

'What did you do then?'

'I started walking. I went north and into the mountains and after a few months I arrived, exhausted and nearly starved to death, at San Petrus. They took me in and cared for my body, and for the first time ever, somebody also cared for my soul. It made a deep impression and I realised that was where I belonged.'

Alcuin had done what he could to get Galen more comfortable with Carbo, but he knew it would take a while. In the meantime he went back to the scenery which was astonishing even after all this time. Alcuin found himself amazed at the grandeur of nature: the high cliffs, the lush valleys, the waterfalls and forests. Around every bend was a new vista. In this kingdom, much of it seemed to still be wilderness where the towns and villages were more sparsely scattered than at home. They'd walked through one village with the houses built from the local stone, and the people had come out to watch them but hadn't engaged with the strangers. And as the little group was fully supplied, there was no need to ask for alms.

Not that it would be easy. The people talking amongst themselves, and the children following the strangers from a safe distance, spoke a dialect that seemed to differ even from what they had heard at the monastery.

'What do you think? Alcuin said, turning to Galen.

'Of what?' Galen asked.

'The language. It's changed so much in such a short distance.'

'Aye,' Carbo said. 'It's like that around here. It seems every valley has its own dialect.'

'Won't that make it difficult to beg for alms?' Alcuin said while shooing away a dog that was sniffing interestedly at his sack of supplies.

'I can make myself understood. It doesn't take much. A monk standing by the side of the road, or in the town square, holding out his hands will get us some food. Although I'm afraid my size puts us at a disadvantage.'

'Ah,' Alcuin said and looked meaningfully at Galen, hoping he'd feel some sympathy for Carbo. 'I suppose one look at you and they reckon you'll gobble up half their hard-earned harvest.'

'That's it. But still, grudging as it often is, the people respect the church and will almost always provide some alms.'

'Thank God for that,' Alcuin said with a big smile, hoping Carbo would seem more human to Galen.

But for the rest of the day Alcuin noticed that Galen always kept out of Carbo's reach. His preference was to keep Alcuin between the two of them.

When the light began to fail and forced them to stop, Galen, despite being exhausted from his day's walk, was jittery and monosyllabic and unwilling to be drawn into conversation. It also shocked Alcuin to discover, when he woke up for his shift on guard late into the night, that Galen was still wide awake, even though it had been Carbo's turn to keep watch.

'What are you doing?' Alcuin whispered once he was certain that Carbo was asleep.

'Nothing,' Galen said with a shudder.

'He won't attack you. I've been watching him. When we passed through those two villages he was eyeing up all the young women in a most unmonk-like manner.'

'I can't,' Galen said, shaking his head. 'I can't trust him.'

'Well, get some sleep now. I'm on guard. I'll make sure nothing happens to you.'

The journey wore away at Galen and the pain grew with every step. He'd have been far more relaxed and less prone to the pain if it was only him and Alcuin, but Carbo was ever present. Not only that, but Alcuin continued to keep his secret which, was so unlike him. It unsettled Galen even more.

He wasn't oblivious to what Alcuin was trying to do though. He knew that his friend kept chatting to Carbo to make him less of a stranger. And it was working to a degree. At least now, three days into their journey, Galen could sleep when it wasn't his turn to be on guard. He couldn't bring himself to interact with Carbo yet though.

It was a bit puzzling even to himself. How could his mind be sensible, but his heart still fill with fear. Carbo's size intimidated him, as did his gruff way of speaking. The fact that he'd been a soldier and engaged in battle was also off-putting. His lack of intellectual curiosity was even more uncomfortable.

Galen never knew what to do with men that were all brawn and little brain. Even Carbo's theology, if you could call it that, was of the simplest kind. He believed in God and prayed to Him in the manner prescribed by the church, end of story.

He'd had no education in his lord's army; yet another detail winkled out of him by Alcuin. He could neither read nor write, and he had no interest in theological debate. Although, in fairness, Alcuin wasn't that keen either, but he could and would go on at length about drawing and all the details he noticed, which always interested Galen.

'There aren't many people about,' Alcuin said, breaking in on Galen's rumination. 'Is this normal?'

Carbo nodded and said, 'It's hard living in the mountains. There's more villages and towns along the large rivers and by the coast. Do you miss people?'

'There's safety in numbers, isn't there?' Alcuin said. 'When we travelled to Lundenburh, we joined a group of merchants and pilgrims. It kept us safe from marauders.'

'It's unlikely here. We aren't on a pilgrim route and there isn't so much trade that it would attract merchant trains. On the other hand, there's slim pickings for robbers here too, so we are less likely to be attacked.'

'That's good to know at least. By the way, Carbo, who is your favourite saint?' Alcuin asked, and Galen recognised it as a desire to keep the conversation going.

Carbo actually stopped and scratched his head as he considered.

'I like the simple men of God,' Carbo said. 'Like the apostles. I suppose Saint Peter would be my favourite. He started life as a fisherman, but then was called by Jesus, dropped everything and followed Him.'

'He is a worthy patron for certain, although I'd have thought you might choose somebody like Saint Sebastian who was also a soldier and is the patron of all soldiers.'

'Also a good man,' Carbo said, nodding thoughtfully.

Galen assumed Carbo had chosen Saint Peter since he was the patron saint of his monastery. It was fair enough, but just seemed to display his lack of interest in looking beyond the obvious.

'I wouldn't go for one of the posh saints,' Carbo said, continuing a conversation Galen had thought had ended before it even began.

'A posh saint? Alcuin said with a laugh. 'What do you mean by that?'

Galen could guess. Carbo had already made it plain that he didn't like the nobility, yet another point where he was an uncomfortable opposite.

'Well... meaning no disrespect, for I can tell the two of you come from well-to-do families,' Carbo said, 'but there's a lot of saints who came from wealth, rose to become bishops or abbots and then were made saints. I'm not saying they weren't worthy, but they... didn't really work for it, did they?'

Alcuin laughed and said, 'I've never really thought much about it. The saints I am most familiar with are those from our own land. Saint Bede is my favourite. I don't know anything of his family, for he went to a monastery at a young age. He was a holy man as well as an intellectual, so it's natural that he became an abbot.'

'Ah, well, learned people like you are bound to be drawn to that kind of a saint.'

Carbo's words were punctuated by a loud rumble from his belly.

'Ah, you're hungry and we're out of supplies,' Alcuin said. 'I knew it was a bad idea to split our food into three equal parts. You should have had a larger helping.'

Galen agreed, but hadn't dared to point it out over the last few days, although both Alcuin and Carbo looked to have lost weight on this journey. It was hard to tell with himself, for he'd always been thin and light.

'Nonsense,' Carbo said. 'I am used to going days without food. This is nothing. Besides, I see a village in the valley, we can just get some food from them.'

Galen supposed another difference between him and Carbo was his willingness to beg for food. Galen had never had to do so. He came from a lordly home, and the Abbey of Yarmwick was a wealthy one. True, at times the variety or quantity of food was somewhat lacking, especially in the hungry gap in the spring where the winter supplies were practically exhausted and the new crops had yet to ripen. But he'd never starved. That was something to mull over and pray thanks to God for. So he had learned something from Carbo after all.

Now the village was so close that they could make out the people and their animals and the strange effect their approach was having. The women and children ran out to gather up their chickens and a pair of boys pulled hard on a rope they'd tied around a pig's neck to drag it away and out of sight. A handful of five men, four of whom were clutching farm implements such as forks and sickles, accompanied by their hunting dogs, blocked the road. Their faces were hard and uncompromising.

'What do you want?' asked the oldest of the men, who was sporting an impressive drooping moustache.

Galen guessed he must be a priest, for three reasons. First, he spoke Latin. Second, he was the only man who wasn't carrying a makeshift weapon, although his rolled-up sleeves showed impressively muscled arms. Finally, he wore robes rather than workman-like clothes.

'We are just a group of monks passing through. If you could spare us some food, we—'

'No!' the man said in an implacable tone. 'There will be no alms from this village.'

'But why not?' Carbo said, looking and sounding astonished. 'Why would you behave so cruelly to travellers in need of food and shelter?'

'We must first look to our own. You may pass through, but there will be no food.'

Galen wondered whether they should bypass the village altogether, rather than risking walking through an unfriendly crowd. But the valley was steep and filled with boulders and brambles, so it would be hard going.

'I could make you regret such words,' Carbo growled, and he raised his staff, now held in both hands.

Galen was shocked that Carbo might resort to violence and gasped, 'No!' before he could stop himself.

Carbo spun round to stare at him, so surprised that the red light of anger faded from his eyes.

'If you don't want it, Brother Galen, I won't. But you are in more need of rest and food than I am.'

'I'm fine,' Galen said and wished he could slip into invisibility, or at least sidle behind Alcuin, but he resisted that instinct.

'We will accept safe passage,' Alcuin said, giving the villagers his best reassuring smile.

Galen approved and prayed it appeased the men; the last thing he wanted was to be ambushed. The men stepped aside, but then closed about the three monks as they made their way down the main street. Apparently they were determined they could neither stop nor receive food during their passage. As they reached the end of the village the men backed off, blocking any possibility of re-entry, but thankfully leaving Galen and his companions to continue unmolested. It was a small mercy and Galen breathed a sigh of relief.

'Well that was something,' Alcuin said, letting out a great sigh.

'It was a damned cheek,' Carbo said, his brow pulled into a deep scowl. 'Such unchristian behaviour will come to harm them in the end.'

'I'm sure you are right, but what could have made them so unfriendly?'

Carbo shrugged.

'Really low supplies or bad experience with other travellers, who can say? They'll come to regret it.'

Alcuin nodded and glanced down at Galen, apparently about to ask something, and his expression turned to one of concern.

'Are you alright?'

Galen tried to smile, failed and said, 'I need to stop, I can't go on.'

'I'll make you a tea. At least I still have your medicinal herbs. You'll feel better soon,' Alcuin said and led Galen to the shade of a nearby tree. He eased him to the ground and said, 'Sleep. Carbo and I will keep watch.'

Galen nodded, too tired to argue and, casting a wary eye in Carbo's direction, curled up into a ball and closed his eyes.

Carbo must have assumed he'd fallen asleep because he said in a soft undertone, 'I don't understand. What have I done to deserve such loathing?'

'He doesn't hate you. He's just afraid,' Alcuin said.

It embarrassed Galen to hear his friend making excuses for him. But he had neither the energy nor the will to open his eyes and engage in the conversation. Especially when it was about him and by a man who, in his angry outburst to the villagers, had made Galen uncomfortable about him once again.

'But why is he afraid?' Carbo said. 'You explained he's shy, but this is more.'

'You just need to give him time.'

'God's blood, how much more time does he need? Have I not proved myself a safe friend, bringing food and getting the locals to give us shelter? What more can I do?'

Alcuin sighed and said, 'I'm sorry, I can't tell you the reason Galen fears you, but believe me, it is a good one. And if you continue to be trustworthy and give Galen time to get used to you, then he will eventually accept you.'

CHAPTER 10

Alcuin had expected a long journey, but today he felt like their trek would never end. They were currently walking along a forested path so narrow they couldn't walk abreast. Carbo was leading the way and his vast bulk blocked the view ahead, adding to the monotony. All Alcuin had to look at was Carbo's vast black-robed back and trees in a variety of greens shading to yellow as autumn took hold. At least they were heading downhill.

Galen continued to be wary of Carbo and still couldn't relax sufficiently to sleep when it wasn't his turn to stand watch, which worried Alcuin. But at least Galen would pass a remark about the countryside through which they were passing to both Alcuin and Carbo.

Most of the time he remained silent though. He wasn't so unkind as to deliberately exclude Carbo from conversation by sticking to Englisc. On top of that, he needed most of his energy for the walking.

Although Carbo had said they were heading out of the mountains, and they had travelled for a couple of weeks already, they were still in hilly terrain. True, the vast snow-capped peaks seemed to have receded somewhat, but they were still a formidable presence.

'We're heading for Foix,' Carbo said, looking back as they wended their way down the side of a bulbous mountain. 'They have an abbey, so we can be sure of a decent meal there.'

'And a roof over our heads,' Alcuin said as his spirits lifted. 'And people who will understand us.'

'It's a relief, isn't it?' Galen said, looking up from his fierce concentration on the path to give Alcuin a smile.

He looked too pale, and more curled over than usual.

'We'll rest a few days there as well,' Alcuin said.

'That would be good.'

Alcuin nodded and gave Galen a searching look. He'd been willing to push on at all their previous stops, so he must have been feeling terrible to be willing to stop for an extended rest. Alcuin decided against making too much of it. People fussing over his illness embarrassed Galen.

Maybe to stave off a too close observation of his person, Galen said, 'It is a relief to be able to stop off at monasteries along the way.'

'That it is,' Alcuin said in wholehearted agreement. 'They are little islands of familiarity dotted about a sea of strangers.'

'In truth, we are the strangers.'

'I know,' Alcuin said, considering the monastery and a church that had provided shelter along their journey so far. 'And the Latin of the brothers we met had an accent and some of the food had an unfamiliar flavour, but all the rest was blessedly similar. The buildings, the rhythm of the day, the prayers, the reading of the rules at dinner. I never knew how comforting it was to be amongst our own kind when we were so far from home.'

'It is the blessing of being in our order,' Carbo said. 'And it makes travelling across the lands of Christendom that much easier.'

'It is an advantage I never considered before,' Galen said. 'I just took it for granted that monasteries exist and that we sometimes had brothers visit us from near and far.'

'But now we see everything in a new light,' Alcuin said, his enthusiasm building. 'Even more so to be visiting an abbey. These bigger institutions often have hospitals with an infirmarius who may be able to supply us with medicines, and a scriptorium. I don't propose we stay long enough to be dragged into work, but to just smell the vellum and inks of a scriptorium will lift my spirits.'

'Poor Alcuin,' Galen said, patting his arm, 'you miss painting, don't you?'

'A bit, but at the moment I am compensating by absorbing all the surrounding images.'

'We should see if we can get you a pencil and some vellum, so you can at least record these things for future use.'

'We'll see.'

Alcuin had already turned down Galen's offer to use his book because he didn't want to deprive Galen of his notebook. He had his doubts any monastery would give them such a precious commodity as vellum, especially if it was bound, and they didn't have sufficient money to buy such an item.

'Ah!' Carbo said and stopped so abruptly that Alcuin bumped into him.

He peered around the monk's vast bulk and understood the dismay in Carbo's voice. Through a gap in the trees, he could see a thick column of black smoke rising into the air.

'What do you think's happened?'

'Nothing good.'

'What is it?'

Galen's voice sounded soft and tired. He hadn't even tried to see what the other two were looking at.

'A fire,' Carbo said. 'A big one, exactly where we're headed.'

He didn't have to spell it out: the town was ablaze, which meant either misfortune or war. It felt like the last straw to Alcuin, who wanted to drop to the ground and wail his frustration. But he couldn't, not when Carbo and Galen were being so stoic. Maybe they felt the same, so for each other's sakes, they were maintaining their calm.

'What should we do?'

Carbo looked around, his lips moving in thought.

'You wait here. I'll find out what's happening. Hide for now, just in case, and don't show yourselves to anyone but me.'

Alcuin nodded and watched until Carbo disappeared beyond some trees. Then he heaved a great sigh.

'So much for a warm dinner and a comfortable bed tonight.'

'I was looking forward to it too,' Galen said and gave Alcuin a slight wan smile that was clearly intended to say he was alright.

Alcuin didn't believe it.

'Let's at least try to find somewhere dry to wait this out,' he muttered.

This was easier said than done. The autumn rains had started, sometimes just a fine misty drizzle, but they'd had a few downpours as well. It left the ground in the forest permanently damp. All the same, some searching got them to a rocky outcrop where one of the grey slabs jutted horizontally out of the ground and provided sufficient shelter for them to squat on the dry earth beneath.

It felt like an age passed as Galen and Alcuin sat under the rock. A light drizzle washed over them. It was blown away by a wind that shook the trees, sending autumn leaves spiralling downwards and adding a second covering to an already thick pile. So it took quite some effort for Galen to navigate his way up to their rocky shelter.

He would have liked nothing better than to rest, but the thought that they could be caught up in the middle of a war, or perhaps just a raid, unsettled him and made it impossible to close his eyes.

'Brother Galen, Brother Alcuin,' came Carbo's voice, drifting through the forest.

'Wait here,' Alcuin said. 'I want to make sure he's alone. It isn't uncommon to use a hostage to lure out others.'

'Be careful,' Galen whispered and wished Alcuin hadn't said what he had. He'd never even considered such a risk and felt foolish to have been so slow. Perhaps it was because of the pain, and, since they'd been sitting still in the cold, his cramping legs.

Thankfully, Alcuin reappeared with Carbo right behind, both looking serious but not worried.

'What happened?'

'Cultists,' Carbo said.

He was never particularly wordy, but this was a new record. He also looked more put out than Galen expected. Alcuin helped Galen to his feet, and taking his weight, got him back to the path.

'You'll need to explain.'

Carbo nodded but waited until they had walked to a clearing where they could look across a river at a smouldering town in the valley below. It was the largest town Galen and Alcuin had seen so far, filling the narrow flat land at the intersection of two rivers. A castle built on a towering cliff loomed over everything and appeared unscathed.

All the damage had occurred in the town. Galen hoped that at least the people had made it up to the fort for safety. There were no flames still visible in the town, so it appeared the locals had got the blaze under control. The only building that was still sending a black plume into the air was an abbey, directly below the fort.

'Oh no,' Alcuin murmured.

'I have been told that a cult came through the town,' Carbo said. 'Led by one Geoffroi the Heretic. He and his people left after a wild battle.'

'Perhaps we should avoid the town. They'll not want strangers there now, and the abbey is unlikely to be able to put us up for the night,' Alcuin said.

'I considered that. But actually, it might be safer to remain in the town. The heretic is unlikely to return, but he is abroad in the land and we need to know where he's headed so we can avoid him.'

He had a point and, much as Galen wanted to stay away from a town that had been ravaged, it looked like they had no choice.

Chapter 11

The trio entered the town on the side that hadn't been attacked and where, aside from an eerie quiet, everything looked fine. But as they continued through the deserted streets, they came to the smouldering heart: a town square directly below the fort on the cliff above. The church looked to be intact, but the front of one of the abbey's other buildings was a smoking wreck. The town on the other half of the narrow square was burnt, and smoke rose in wisps from the blackened ruins.

Galen came to a shuddering halt as he noticed a body curled up against the wall of a house, with its hands over its head in a protective posture. Thick dark red blood pooled about it, diluted at the edges by the rain.

'Dear God, protect us,' Galen whispered as he made a sign of the cross over the body and commended the man's soul up to God.

'Who are you?' an angry voice shouted, and a group of people, mainly monks, but with some townspeople amongst them, came running.

They were brandishing an assortment of makeshift weapons: a pitchfork here, a kitchen knife there, and many wooden buckets that would cause serious damage if smashed against a man's head.

'Peace,' Carbo said, holding up his hands.

Galen doubted it would have a calming effect. Carbo appeared more like a bear now, on his hind legs and making himself tall and wide, but it did stop the hostile crowd.

'I beg your pardon,' Alcuin said in Latin, coming up beside Carbo, 'we are but monks in need of shelter for the night.'

'What proof do you have of that?' a thin, middle-aged monk said as he pushed his way through the knot of men.

His habit was plain, and he didn't have the look of the leader of an order, but he had an air of command, especially amongst this rag-tag bunch.

Alcuin waved at Galen, Carbo and himself and said, 'My brothers and I have travelled far. Brother Galen and I are from Engla-lond. We are on our way to Rome.'

'A likely story,' a voice muttered from the crowd. It had to be one of the monks, for he was also speaking Latin.

'We don't expect something for nothing. We will do our part and help where we can, for we can see that we have arrived at an inauspicious time.'

'Inauspicious?!' the middle-aged monk said. 'Is it in the nature of your people to make such understatements?'

'I suppose it is,' Alcuin said with a wry laugh.

Trust Alcuin to win people over, Galen thought, watching him with pride. They were already halfway there with the man's tacit acceptance of where they'd come from.

'How do we know you aren't from Geoffroi the Heretic's cursed band?'

'Until today, we'd never even heard of this Geoffroi. What exactly happened here?'

There was some muttering amongst the group, and the scowls of the townsfolk deepened, possibly because they recognised the name of their attacker.

'You've never heard of Geoffroi the Heretic?' the lead monk said, and he sounded surprised. 'You really aren't from these parts.'

'As I said,' Alcuin said in his most pleasant voice, working to be as non-threatening as possible.

'Geoffroi used to be a priest, a well liked one at that,' the monk started, then was shouted at by one of the townspeople.

The man sounded impatient, and the monk spent some time with a shouted back and forth, which resulted in all but the thin monk heading back to the burned remains of the building. Galen realised with a shocked twist of his stomach that they were carrying bodies from the smouldering wreck into the church.

'There's the body of a monk just down this street.'

Galen hadn't intended to whisper, but that was all that came out.

The monk gave him a sharp look, as if noticing him for the first time. His suspicious bearing also returned.

'How do you know?'

'We... came in that way,' Galen said.

'Are you ill?' the monk asked, his wariness increasing.

'He's just exhausted. We've walked for many days,' Alcuin said while putting his body between Galen and the monk. 'Perhaps we could speak to your abbot?'

The monk laughed. It was harsh, nearly hysterical.

'Our abbot is dead, along with our infirmarius and more than half of our brothers.'

'Good Lord, why? How?' Alcuin gasped.

'Because the heretic has taken it into his head that all men of the cloth must either join him or be executed. He claimed our religious orders have taken the wrong path and God has sent him to rectify that. Geoffroi and his growing band have washed across the land, pillaging every town they've come to in the name of redistribution. He claims it's to feed his hungry followers, but it's nothing of the sort. Geoffroi grows fat while his followers stay as ragged and lean as the wild beasts he has turned them into. All the spoils go to the heretic, including the women.'

'Why would anyone follow such a man?' Galen said, so shocked he couldn't stop himself.

'Why indeed? He has an overpowering presence, that is certain. Geoffroi is a big man with wild, flowing hair and a silver tongue. He came in saying he wanted to preach a sermon and before we could ask more, he'd set to proselytising on the steps of the church.

'The entire town came out to see what the roaring man had to say. His followers spread themselves out amongst the people, cheering his every word. They were waving their arms about and singing God's praises upon Geoffroi's urging. I will admit it was a moving experience to see so many swept up in the ecstasy of prayer.'

'And then?' Carbo said, his voice heavy with disapproval.

The monk looked back at the wreckage and the line of people taking bodies into the church across the blood and ash strewn square.

'Then he demanded that we, all of us, the monks and the townspeople, renounce the church and follow him. He claimed to be a prophet, speaking for God. He said that God ordered us to give up all our worldly goods and follow him.'

'Typical!' Carbo snorted.

'That's when our abbot intervened. He and all the senior members of our abbey had gathered at our door to watch the spectacle. Our abbot roared at Geoffroi that he was nothing more than a heretic. And Geoffroi shouted back that all in the church were degenerates.

'Then, without warning, his people rushed the abbey, swept away the abbot and set fire to everything. I expected the townspeople to stand with us, but the heretic had already swayed some and they joined in on the attack against the abbey. I have never seen a more horrific sight than brother turned against brother, neighbour against neighbour,' the monk said, and his face twisted in pain.

Galen was so shocked by this tale that he felt shaky and wished the monk would stop.

'But you saw him off,' Carbo said.

'We managed somehow, although many of our people went with him. Some went voluntarily but some, the women especially, were just dragged away.'

'It's as well you fought him. I've heard of cult leaders who like to set themselves up as rulers of a town and have all who live there serve him. It may not seem like it, but you won a victory by forcing him out.'

'Not as much of a victory as you think,' the monk said, rubbing the back of his neck ruefully. 'From what he was saying in his rabble-rousing speech, he intends to take over Toulouse.'

'But that's the seat of a powerful count, is it not?'

'Not anymore. It's ruled by a viscount of the same family. He split away from the rest and rules Toulouse as his own fiefdom. The same is happening everywhere. The king is far away and powerless. Each town and city is hunkered down, relying on local warlords for protection. It's a precarious situation and one where Geoffroi the Heretic will be able to take whatever he wants.'

Carbo grunted and shook his head at the parlous state of the world.

'Things really are looking bad. However, Brother Alcuin and I are fit and able to help you with the clean up. Brother Galen will find somewhere to rest.'

'A big man like you will be a help indeed,' the monk said, looking the trio over yet again. 'I'm Brother Johanne, by the way.'

'So, are you in charge?'

'I suppose I am the most senior monk left standing. Until the bishop sends us a new abbot, I suppose I am in charge.'

'I can write,' Galen said and then paused because it was out of context. 'If... if you need any records to be made of the missing and the dead.'

Brother Johanne looked Galen over and said, 'I'm not sure our scriptorium survived. We haven't ventured that deeply into the abbey yet. We've been clearing the square and the streets. If you and your angelic-looking friend want to take a look, I suppose it will be useful to make a record of this day. Help yourself to all you need. I'm afraid our armarius is also amongst the dead. Now I will take your big brother away to do some heavy lifting.'

Galen nodded as he watched the two depart, Carbo giving him an anxious look. Galen, on the other hand, preferred it when Carbo wasn't around.

'That was an excellent suggestion,' Alcuin said as the two of them made their way to the burned entrance of the abbey.

'I'm just relieved that I can be of use. I often wish I could do more than just watch from the sidelines.'

Despite the smouldering beams inside, one of which had collapsed, bringing down half the roof and scattering slates across the floor, the interior was less damaged than they'd expected and appeared to have been a refectory with a now charred table running the full length of the room. A pair of monks were carrying out the last body and eyed them suspiciously.

Alcuin and Galen gave the men a bow and then they headed to the back of the refectory, where a door led into a kitchen. A fire was still smouldering under the large black cauldron.

'Pottage,' Alcuin said, peering inside. 'I'll just put out the fire so the food doesn't dry up and burn. Hopefully, some of that will turn into our dinner.'

'I'm not really hungry anymore,' Galen said, resting his weight on his staff as Alcuin stamped on the fire.

'That's understandable. I'm relieved we arrived after the heretic though. Thank God we weren't caught up in the riot itself.'

Galen nodded and took Alcuin's arm again as they left the kitchen and entered a small courtyard. This abbey was considerably smaller than Yarmwick. Because it was built within the narrow valley with its back to a cliff, it was more cramped in design.

The scriptorium was a smallish room with only eight desks. All of them had open books, ink and pens abandoned, as the monks had apparently left in a hurry.

'The heretic upended everything.'

The scribe in Galen winced at the waste of ink as it had started to dry and thicken in the horns.

'How can such a thing come about? How can such extremists exist?' Alcuin said as he led Galen to a chair that must have belonged to the armarius, for there was a stack of writing supplies piled on this desk, some of which had toppled to the floor.

Galen had also been wondering how one man could garner such influence and cause so much chaos.

'These cult leaders must offer something to the people that they don't get from anybody else. Why else would ordinary people, even the local townspeople of what looks like a prosperous and safe community, go off with this Geoffroi?'

'Maybe Carbo is right. Maybe they are lazy and want to live a life of ease.'

'Mmm,' Galen said, looking around the small scriptorium and trying to imagine labouring in it day after day and year after year. 'Nobody actually has an easy life. Some might think a king has it easy, but he has constant war and internal conspiracies to deal with. Likewise, monks don't have it as quiet as people believe, and nor do robbers who are often accused of taking the easy route.'

'But people are easily tricked into believing one way or another will be easier, and they'll even follow an out-and-out maniac.'

'And give him their full devotion, by the looks of things. That still suggests a level of desperation to me. One that will blind the follower to their leader's flaws.

'My father once spoke of a thrall who firmly believed my father could do no wrong, no matter what he said or did. It was strange for one who is at the mercy of another, or so my father thought. But since then I have seen more of those kinds of people. Perhaps a cult is one such gathering of desperation.'

'To the point where you'll risk your life in an all out war against your idol's enemies? That is extreme indeed.'

Galen nodded and turned his attention to the desk.

'His method is wrong if he is indeed trying to bring the word of God to the people.'

'There can be no doubt about that.'

Alcuin picked up the three gatherings of vellum that had fallen to the floor, dusted them off and placed them back on the pile.

'But you know...' Galen hesitated over how he phrased this, 'there have been times in our own order's past when men of Christ have been equally violent.'

'Galen, no!' Alcuin said and paused his search through the chest he'd just opened.

'I will say nothing of this when we are with other people,' Galen said, and hoped that reassured Alcuin. He was a friend and confidant and more understanding than most, which was why Galen could say these things. 'Sometimes, when I think about the start of Catholicism, and from what I learned of Islam from Hatim, it doesn't feel... well, it doesn't feel so different to some cults.'

Alcuin gasped.

'You'd better not say that to anyone else.'

'I won't.' Galen had known it would shake Alcuin, and that he regretted. The thought actually left him feeling uncomfortable too. 'This gathering, a horn of ink and a handful of pens should be sufficient for the records. Should we go back to the church now?'

'I fear it will be a gruesome job,' Alcuin said.

'But it has to be done,' Galen said and took a deep breath to prepare himself.

CHAPTER 12

Two weeks had passed since their stop in Foix. The monks and the townsfolk had worked hard to clean and repair the town and get back to some semblance of order. But when Galen, Alcuin and Carbo decided to leave, there was still much to do.

Galen had handed over his meticulous list of the dead: their names, occupations and ages, along with a brief description of what had happened on that fateful day. It had surprised him how many people came to sit beside him in the church to tell him their tale. It was all much as Brother Johanne had described it, but still the people came.

As he walked, Galen got the sense that it gave them some comfort to talk about it, much as a trip to the confessional relieved the soul of its burdens. Their need to speak, and the violence of the cult, preoccupied Galen. But, mainly because walking required so much effort, and a bit because he'd shocked Alcuin when he'd talked about the cult's similarity to their order, he kept his ruminations to himself.

That was when he wasn't so tired that he sank into a daze, where dreamlike, incoherent images drifted across his mind. He was plodding in one such daze now. He was relieved that at least, after a sustained climb all morning, they were headed downhill again.

Alcuin gave a start, came to a stop and shouted, 'Look, look, it's the sea!'

It took some effort to look up, but it was worth it. Far below, down the winding track, was an inky blue sea that stretched to the horizon.

'We made it,' Alcuin said, grinning at Galen. 'The Mediterranean.'

'We did,' Galen murmured, and he stared at the sea as if it were a miracle.

Perhaps it was. Or at least the fact that they had made it this far was the miracle. It had been such a long walk that the leaves were almost all yellow now and the weather had become considerably wetter. Heavy rain showers punctuated the journey, saturating the ground and forcing the travellers to take cover, since Alcuin was unwilling to risk Galen's health by letting him get soaked.

'And I walked all the way,' Galen said. 'I wouldn't have believed it possible.'

'You did well. You're walking faster too, and you've developed a healthy tan.'

'All thanks to Hatim. I couldn't have walked this distance before.'

'That's true, but you're still in pain, aren't you?'

'When I wake from a night's rest, I feel almost nothing. But after walking all day, it can get pretty bad.'

'It might be a bit better if you slept through the night more often and just took the first shift of watching like you should,' Alcuin said, casting a meaningful glance towards Brother Carbo.

Galen shook his head and his eyes flicked to the monk's vast form as he strolled a little way ahead of them.

'He has respected your feelings and hasn't gone near you. I believe he is to be trusted.'

'Maybe.'

Galen knew full well that Carbo wasn't Septimus and that he was unlikely to attack him. He felt guilty that he avoided him, but they were not compatible. There was also something off about the man's behaviour. He was more obsequious than necessary and had shown flashes of temper that made Galen uncomfortable.

Alcuin was also hiding why Carbo was with them. Something, weeks later, he still hadn't disclosed. It all added to Galen's disquiet.

'You could at least try speaking to him. He's feeling like an outcast the way you kee—'

The ground gave way under their feet and they fell, rolling and churning in a blurred confusion of a world upended. Galen landed in a stream with a splash as earth and rocks rushed down on top of him. Then Carbo landed on Galen with a heavy thump, knocking out all remaining air.

'Ooof!' Carbo cried and wallowed about, crushing Galen as the big monk tried to right himself.

'Get off me!' Galen screamed and pushed against him, sobbing in panic, his breathing heavy and fast. 'Get off me!'

Carbo hauled himself up, showering Galen with wet clods of earth.

'Are you alright, Brother Galen?'

Galen gave him a white-faced, frightened look, then realised something awful. He was alone with the big man.

'Alcuin..? Where's Alcuin?'

Galen pushed himself onto his hands and knees with all the strength he had as his eyes darted about. He was shaking and unsteady as he took in the fan of soil around them, dotted with rocks. Then he spotted a fragment of black cloth poking out from the mud.

'Alcuin!' Galen cried as he scrambled to his feet and staggered forward, sinking knee deep into the mud, moving painfully slowly. Alcuin was face down in the dirt. Galen pulled at Alcuin's robe and dug frantically about his body to turn him over.

'Alcuin, can you hear me?' Galen gasped, wiping the mud off his friend's face.

Alcuin was unusually pale, and his eyes remained shut. But worst was the deep gash to his forehead that oozed blood and obscured half of his face.

'Dear God, help me!' Galen gasped.

Carbo came wading up and leaned over Galen.

'He's been hit on the head. It looks bad.'

Galen started and, despite knowing it would do no good, scuttled to Alcuin's other side to keep Carbo away from his back. Then, keeping his eyes on Alcuin, he pulled open the sack that was still strapped to Alcuin's body and scrabbled about in it till he found the vial which held the poppy syrup Hatim had given him. Thankfully, it was still in one piece.

He dripped a couple of drops into Alcuin's mouth, praying all the time. He felt sick with anxiety. He couldn't lose Alcuin. His mind shut down at the possibility.

'We should get him out of the mud,' Carbo said.

'No!' Galen said sharply. 'We can't move him.'

'He's wet. Let me carry him up to higher ground.'

Galen looked up the slope to where the landslide had wiped away the path. Now there was just a gaping hole and a smear of earth all the way down to them.

'No, he mustn't be moved.'

'But honestly, Brother Galen, I will be gentle. He won't be hurt. But you can't leave him here. The stream will wear away at this earth and reclaim its path which will be right over Alcuin.'

'We can't move him. Not until tomorrow.'

Galen's heart was jumping in his throat with fear. Fear of losing Alcuin and fear of having to face Carbo down.

'You don't look too well yourself,' Carbo said. 'You're shaking.'

'I'll be fine.'

Galen hoped Carbo didn't notice the way he was clenching his fists to fight against the excruciating pain. His body had been wrenched by the fall and having the entire mass of Brother

Carbo land on top of him. He was bruised and shaken, but he didn't have time to think of his own woes.

'What can I do to help?' Carbo asked.

Galen looked at him blankly, trying to think. Alcuin was incapable of taking matters in hand. He was the one who needed help.

'Can you divert the stream so it doesn't flow back this way, then we'll be alright. And maybe make some sort of shelter over Alcuin.'

'You sure you don't want to move him?'

'Yes, I'm sure' Galen said with conviction, even though his voice shook.

Carbo looked from Galen, who felt on the verge of tears, to the dangerously pale Alcuin.

'Do you know what you are doing?'

'Only in so far as it's been done for me. I can tell you, not moving him is for the best.'

'Very well, I'll work on the stream first,' Carbo said and started hunting around for something to use as a tool.

Galen clung on to Alcuin's cold, wet hand while he tried to clean his friend's face with his other, praying all the time to God for help. He was so focused on this that he barely noticed Carbo.

By dusk Carbo had made an island of the mound of earth Alcuin rested on and had built a shelter from the branches and leaves of the nearby trees.

Despite his greater fears, Galen still jumped if Carbo approached him from behind. Maybe the big monk was aware of it, because after a while he only approached from the front.

Now he clambered over the loose earth, carrying a hunk of bread and said, 'Do you want something to eat, Brother Galen?'

Galen, kneeling as he had been all day by Alcuin's side, shook his head.

Carbo nodded and paused to examine Alcuin.

'He doesn't look good. That swelling around his head wound has grown and I don't like the way it's turning dark.'

Galen wanted to scream at him to shut up. He didn't want to be told something he could see with his own eyes and that made him sick to the pit of his stomach. Then a shudder ran through Alcuin. He twitched so violently his hand slipped from Galen's grasp and flecks of foam flew from his mouth.

'Alcuin!' Galen shouted and tried to hold his friend still.

'Not good,' Carbo murmured. 'I've seen this before. Death throes.'

'Help me turn him over,' Galen shouted, too worried about Alcuin to pay heed to Carbo. 'I must get him onto his side so he doesn't choke on this spit.'

'I don't think there's much p—'

'Help me!' Galen screamed as he pulled frantically at Alcuin's still half-buried body.

'Alright,' Carbo said and slid his two gigantic hands under Alcuin and rolled him over.

Galen tugged at Alcuin's arms and legs. He could feel the seizure through his hands. All the same, he got Alcuin into the position he wanted and clung desperately to his body as it shuddered and shook. Carbo retreated to a respectful distance.

Despite wanting to ignore Carbo's words, Galen had seen death often enough to know that Alcuin was beyond what his meagre medicines and rest could cure. The panic that numbed his limbs threatened to rise up and overwhelm him, turning his body to lead. He couldn't allow this. He couldn't live if Alcuin died here.

'Oh merciful God,' he prayed, putting more force into this prayer than he had ever done in his life, 'please, if I am a saint, if I am worthy of anything from You, please use Your power to heal Alcuin. He has sinned, but he has always tried his best to serve

You. And his art, oh God, please don't take his art away from the world just yet. Please God, if I had anything to bargain with, I would. If You want me instead of him, take me. The world will be no poorer for the lack of a single scribe.'

Alcuin's trembling subsided and Galen opened his eyes, fearing the worst, but hoping for a miracle. Hope was dashed as he saw Alcuin's face as pale and still as death, the terrible wound to his head as swollen and blackened as ever.

Galen pushed himself onto his knees. He put his right hand gently over the wound whilst his left was curled up tight against his body, holding in the pain and the shriek of grief that was on the verge of escaping. He prayed, over and over again, pleading with God, bargaining and interspersing it with prayers from his childhood, the only things his disturbed mind could dredge up.

For hour after hour, as the sun set, as the clouds blew over, obscuring the moon, as the rain fell, and the wind blew it away and the trees tossed about, making the stars blink in and out of existence, he prayed.

As the sun rose across the hills that marched to the sea, and the land lit up in the soft colours of dawn, Carbo threw off his cloak, stretched his cramped limbs and made his way over to Galen. Galen noted all of that in the back of his mind as he bent over Alcuin, rocking back and forth, his lips moving in silent and perpetual prayer.

'Is he still alive?' Carbo asked.

His voice was hesitant, but as one who didn't want to offend rather than one who believed Alcuin was still with them. Galen was so numb he couldn't move, and no sound escaped his throat, although his prayers continued.

'Brother Galen,' Carbo said and dropped to his knees on the other side of Alcuin. Neither of them looked down. Galen didn't dare to, for fear of what he would see. 'You can't stay here forever. Let me take care of this now. I will make sure he is properly buried.'

Galen understood, but couldn't move even if he'd wanted to, which he didn't. To move now would be to acknowledge the terrible truth.

Alcuin coughed, opened his eyes and looked around in a befogged way.

'Holy Mary, Mother of God!' Carbo said and stumbled back, then tripped on a rock and fell on his behind.

His gaze remained locked on Alcuin as he crossed himself once and then again, and again. Alcuin laughed. What was wrong with the man? Then he realised Galen was leaning over him, his eyes wide in blank amazement.

'You're alright!' Galen gasped.

'Of course I'm alright. Why wouldn't I be? And why are the two of you hovering around me like this and why… why am I sitting upon an enormous pile of mud?'

'It's a miracle!' Carbo said. 'There isn't a mark on you.'

Alcuin gave him a puzzled look and turned to examine the white-faced Galen.

'What is he talking about? What happened?'

'The road collapsed,' Galen said and waved his hand vaguely upwards.

'Are you alright?' Alcuin asked, instantly alarmed. 'You aren't hurt, are you? Not bleeding?'

'I'm fine.' Galen burst into tears and wrapped his arms about Alcuin, his shoulders heaving as he muttered, 'Thank God, thank God,' in a hoarse voice.

'Now what's going on?' Alcuin asked as he gently pushed Galen back.

'I've said it once and I'll say it again: it's a blessed miracle,' Carbo said. 'And Galen must be a saint. He cured you, and Fra' Arnal dreamed he was blessed, and so he is. It's the only explanation.'

Alcuin, by this time, had assimilated his surroundings, noticing the makeshift shelter and that all of them were covered in mud. Now he was trying to wrack his memory to work out how he'd got there.

'I have a feeling I need some explanation.'

'Well, that's an understatement and no mistake,' Carbo said with a grin.

Alcuin looked back at Galen, trying to work out why he was so overwrought. He eased Galen's arms away and noted that his left hand was curled into a fist. Alcuin gently prised his fingers open and was unsurprised to see that Galen was bleeding from the cuts his nails had dug into the flesh.

'I haven't seen that in a long time.'

Alcuin put an arm around Galen's waist, pulled them both to their feet and guided the sobbing youth along the narrow valley, out of the mud and to a dry patch under a pine tree. He got Galen to sit, then settled beside him, worried by his shivering and more determined than ever to find out what had happened.

'Carbo, you'd better tell me.'

Carbo had followed behind, almost bent double as if in a perpetual bow. He was suddenly subservient to the point where it irritated Alcuin. Something momentous had definitely happened.

'Yesterday, the road gave way as we were walking along it,' Carbo said, and waved his hand in the direction of the landslip. 'We all came crashing down, but you... you were hit a mighty blow by a rock. Your head was broken, blood was pouring out. Brother Galen tried to give you medicine and kept you still, but it didn't look good. Your body was shaking, foam was coming out of your mouth.'

Alcuin stared in amazement at Carbo and gingerly ran his fingers over his temple. It felt fine. There was no sign of such a gruesome wound.

'Brother Galen prayed for you,' Carbo said, his voice soft with awe. 'All night. He never left your side. He just prayed and prayed and now look. You're better. Perfectly healed; not even a scar.'

'Galen, is this true?'

Alcuin found it hard to believe, but at the same time his heart beat uncomfortably fast. Had he really been so near death? Given Carbo and Galen's reactions, he had to believe it was true. It awed him beyond everything he'd seen so far, to believe that Galen had healed him.

'I just... I just prayed.'

'You saved my life!'

'God saved your life. Besides... you... you've saved mine many times,' Galen said jerkily.

'Aye, and by the look of you, I'd better do it again,' Alcuin said. 'You've been thrown about quite a bit, haven't you?'

'I landed on top of him,' Carbo said guiltily.

Alcuin's eyes widened in dismay.

'Did he?'

Galen nodded.

'Then you must be a mass of bruises and if you didn't sleep last night, you must be ready to drop. So lie down.'

'Don't leave me,' Galen said and clutched Alcuin's arm.

'I won't. I'll stay right here whilst you sleep and be right here when you wake up. Do we have any of that poppy syrup left, by the way?'

'In my bag.'

'Then you'd best have some. You're overwrought. You'll never get to sleep like this.'

Galen gave a relieved, shaky smile and said, 'Thank God you're back, Alcuin.'

Carbo looked at a bit of a loss, hovering beside them.

Then he came to a decision and said, 'I will look for a way out for us. Now that you're up...' He flushed red, shook his head in incredulity and hurried away.

So now Alcuin was alone with his thoughts and they were tumultuous indeed. He gazed up the steep valley slope and tried to remember. But there was nothing, just the memory of walking along the path, and then waking in Galen's arms.

His hand shook, frightened by what it meant, and he clutched Galen's sleeve, tightening his fist around the fabric as he prayed his thanks to God and to His servant Galen. It felt unreal. At moments he wondered whether this gratitude was necessary because it was difficult to believe what had happened as he felt so well.

Far better than when he'd been tired from the walk the day before. That caused another uncomfortable shudder and he sent a flood of more grateful prayers up to heaven.

Why him? He was grateful, of course, but his life was unexceptional and not exactly exemplary. He did his best to illustrate God's creation but he could hardly be called worthy.

It embarrassed him sometimes when Galen spoke so highly of his art. He'd been genuinely shocked when Galen had begged Hatim to only chop *his* hands off and to spare Alcuin's hands for the sake of his art. He loved doing it, of course, but should a man be rewarded for doing something he loved?

Maybe that was what this journey was all about. A penance and a time for learning. He was away from what he loved: his drawing. All around him were sources of inspiration. But he had neither the tools nor the time to do much with it. So what else should he do?

Should he wait until he could return to his art, which felt like it might take years, or find himself another role? No, he didn't even have to look for another role. He already had one, looking after Galen, who, it seemed, really was a saint, and not only because of the miracles.

Chapter 13

Alcuin acted his tyrannical best and forced Galen to rest for three full days before he was willing to consider continuing their journey. Carbo, who'd always been patient with their pace and the number of stops they took, accepted the enforced rest with his usual stolidity. In fact, with more than that. Anything that was now required for Galen became of paramount and overwhelming importance to the point of dogma.

Alcuin found it interesting, even amusing sometimes. Then stopped the smile that touched his lips as he remembered he'd be dead now if it weren't for Galen. It was a difficult concept to come to terms with.

But Galen and Carbo's reaction told him of the momentous event and continued to leave him with mixed feelings. Chief amongst those were an intense gratitude to Galen, shock that death had come so close, and a deep disquiet. He feared what this very real, finally very obvious, miracle meant. It was a mixed blessing, he found, when it should merely have been an event to rejoice over.

Was it significant that such a powerful saint had appeared now? Was the end of the world near? Would the millennium herald the return of Christ?

And what did all of this mean for Galen? How would his life change if people saw him as a bona fide saint? Would he even be able to cope with that, given his fear of strangers?

Galen slept through most of Alcuin's ruminations, but when he was awake, he made no mention of the miracle. He appeared to wish to go on as he always had. That worried Alcuin the most.

How could his friend adapt to this change in his circumstances if he didn't acknowledge it? Alcuin saw trouble ahead for the two of them in Rome. He started wondering whether it wouldn't be better to go straight back home.

He never worked up the courage to suggest that option though and said nothing when Galen woke on the fourth morning and announced that he was ready to go on.

'If you're certain.'

'I'm sick of the sight of those tree branches waving over my head. I yearn for a roof and somewhere to spend the night where the wind isn't howling about us.'

'Well, as Carbo tells me we're near a seaport, I think we can manage that,' Alcuin said with an amused smile as he helped Galen to his feet. 'Although it's going to be a challenge getting back up to the path. This valley is pretty steep. Carbo and I discussed the possibility of continuing along the valley, following the river. While you've been resting he's explored up and down but, unfortunately, it's impassable. So we're going to have to make our way back up to the path.'

Galen took a deep, fortifying breath and was about to speak when a shout came from above them.

'Ahoy there! Can you hear us?' came a voice shouting in blessedly recognisable Latin.

Two heads peered out from the road above, waving their arms to draw attention.

'We can hear you!' Alcuin shouted, waving back. 'Can you help us back up?'

'I'm sure we can,' one man shouted. 'My friend will go back to the village we passed and borrow some rope. Just give us some time.'

'Thank God,' Alcuin said, beaming at Galen.

He hadn't wanted to trouble his friend, but he'd been worrying about how they would get out of the valley. He and Carbo could probably manage it, but it would have been a struggle for Galen.

'I need to call Carbo back. He's been taking longer and longer to get back with food lately. Thank goodness he knows how to forage. Although I'm tiring of mushrooms.'

'Yes,' Galen said noncommittally.

'You still don't trust him?'

'I wonder why he's here and about that dream he mentioned.'

'Oh, you noticed, did you?'

'So you knew about it?'

'I overheard him and Fra' Arnal speaking of it. Carbo doesn't know that I know.'

'But why didn't you tell me?'

Galen glanced up the slope, as if seeing whether the man above was watching or listening.

'Is that what's been bothering you?'

'You rarely keep secrets from me.'

Alcuin felt himself flushing, thinking about the secrets he had kept, and it filled him with guilt.

'Alright, I'll tell you what I heard,' Alcuin said and related Fra' Arnal's dream.

'So that's why Carbo is with us,' Galen said, his brow crinkling into thought.

'It's probably best not to worry about it.'

Alcuin tried to look cheerful, but it was hard to maintain with Galen looking up at him with a worried expression. What he might have said was going to have to wait, though, as Carbo emerged from the bushes at the same time as a long rope slapped down the side of the valley, uncoiling as it went, and stopped, swaying gently, a few feet from Alcuin.

'Good Lord,' Carbo said, his gaze travelling up the rope to the waving men above.

'They appeared a little while ago,' Alcuin said.

'Let me go up first and make sure all is safe. Then I can help haul the two of you up.'

'Oh, I think we can manage on our own.'

'But there is no need to.'

Carbo tugged at the rope, checking how secure it was. Then he pulled himself upwards, hand over hand, walking up the valley wall.

'That should be easy enough for us both, shouldn't it?'

Alcuin felt more awkward than usual with Galen, whose troubled expression was harder to interpret today because it could stem from so many things.

In the end, despite Galen wishing he was robust enough to get himself out of the valley, he and Alcuin tied the rope around themselves, and, with the combined strength of Carbo and what turned out to be two other monks, they were hoisted out of the valley.

'Are you alright?' the younger of the two monks said.

He was tall and slim with sandy reddish hair. His face was tanned, freckled but surprisingly smooth. The other monk was slightly taller, but his face was craggy and deeply lined. They were both wearing threadbare habits so bleached by the sun that they were pale grey, rather than black.

'They're monks, just like us,' Carbo said, beaming as he hoisted Alcuin and Galen up to the path. They'd come up on the seaward side, through the hole that had formed from the landslip.

Gathered on the other side of the gaping hole was a small group consisting of three men, four women and six children. They had the haggard look of people who hadn't eaten for a while, and their clothes were even more threadbare than the monks'.

'We are all headed to Rome. I am Brother Bartolo, and this is Brother Gentile. He has taken a vow of silence,' the younger of the two monks said.

'And what of them?' Carbo said, pointing at the group of laypeople.

'They are pilgrims we gathered along the way.'

'Pilgrims?' Carbo said, with a note of suspicion in his voice.

'People who have fallen upon hard times and are now on a journey to Rome to pray for God's intervention.'

'They could just as easily pray from home.'

'That's assuming they have a home,' Bartolo said with a smile that seemed to say he could debate this point all day and he would eventually win.

A tingle of anxiety ran through Galen that he put down to being among strangers and men who seemed on the verge of an argument.

'If we are to make it to the sea,' Alcuin said, 'perhaps we should continue this conversation as we walk. I'm Brother Alcuin, by the way. This is Brother Galen and Brother Carbo.'

Galen sighed with relief. Trust Alcuin to step in at the crucial moment. He kept Alcuin's solid body between himself and the rest of the party as they resumed walking, although he felt ashamed of himself for being so timid.

The huddle of pilgrims waited until all the monks were already in motion before they made their cautious way in single file along what remained of the road to join the monks. Neither Brother Bartolo nor the silent Brother Gentile paid them any heed, which Galen found strange.

He had little time to consider them though. The sea looked a long way off, but talk was of reaching it by evening. First, they had to get out of these foothills and down into a shallow u-shaped valley with a river running through it.

The largest fields Galen had seen since leaving the Monastery of San Petrus dotted the valley. Unkempt fruit trees grew alongside a few fields of cabbages. The lush grazing held only a handful of goats, sheep and tan-coloured cows with enormous horns. Someone had already harvested the fields of grain and the remaining stubble was being picked over by humans and birds alike.

'It looks half abandoned,' Galen said, eyeing an empty field that had become overgrown with weeds. 'Look, Alcuin. You'd never see that in Engla-lond.'

'Maybe it's because the land is so vast, there's more than enough to go around,' Alcuin said.

Brother Bartolo snorted at that comment.

'You don't know much, do you? Everyone has fought over this land since Roman times. Just in the last hundred years there were invasions by the Magyars from the east, then the Vikings, and lately the Moors, who swept all the way across to Toulouse. They could probably have taken the city, but, for whatever reason, they pulled back.'

'God stopped them,' Carbo said.

'But only at Toulouse. Apparently He was fine with them taking over Al-Andalus.'

Carbo glared at the man, chewing his lips in impotent fury. He wasn't a debater, and Galen didn't risk saying anything lest he land up agreeing with Bartolo.

That monk gave a triumphant smile.

'As if invasion hasn't been enough of a trial, there has also been a series of disastrous seasons. Sometimes there is too much rain and sometimes too little. On top of that, a plague has swept through, wiping out half the population. Is it any wonder, with all of these signs, the common people are convinced the end times are near?'

Galen disagreed but had no intention of saying so, although Alcuin looked enquiringly down at him as if he wanted his opinion.

'So where are you from?' Carbo asked, looking Brother Bartolo over, like a warrior sizing up his opponent. 'Your Latin has an unfamiliar accent.'

'I am from Rome,' Bartolo said with a smile that implied he would not be easy to pick a fight with.

'Then why are you here?'

'My mistress sent me on a mission.'

'Mistress?'

Carbo's voice rose in volume and pitch, the disapproval increasing.

'Sister Marozia, perhaps you have heard of her?'

'How can you, a member of the Benedictine order, have a mistress?'

'Who said I'm a Benedictine?' Bartolo asked, his voice as level and calm as ever.

This surprised Galen and apparently also Alcuin because he gave a start.

'Your habit,' Carbo said.

'Gentile and I have no other clothes, so the habit remains. But we left the order once we met Sister Marozia.'

'Why would you do such a thing?'

'Our abbot cared more about the sumptuousness of his home and his meals than he did for the souls of his monks and the people in the surrounding land. Everywhere we looked, we saw corruption, and this at such a critical time in history. Then Sister Marozia appeared, preaching the way to live a righteous life. She pointed out that Jesus was poor and lived amongst the people, but monks live in luxury and wall themselves off from everyone.'

As he spoke, he turned to the silent Brother Gentile, who nodded affirmation.

'Many monasteries also feed the hungry and treat the sick,' Carbo said and his face tinged red as his temper became inflamed.

'Does yours?'

'Mine? No. We have removed ourselves from the material world. We take our vow of poverty seriously and we support ourselves entirely with the sweat of our own labour. I doubt there is a single piece of gold in the entire monastery.'

'Then yours is an exception.' Bartolo's gaze drifted over Alcuin and Galen and he said, 'Are you two not from the same monastery?'

'We are from the Abbey of Yarmwick in Engla-lond,' Alcuin said. 'Ours is a large abbey and an influential one. We are mainly financed through the production of books.'

'So you do live in comfort,' Brother Bartolo said, as if it was a clincher.

'I wouldn't exactly call it comfortable.' Galen felt Alcuin's body tense. He could understand it. He also felt insulted by the way this monk dismissed them. 'We live better than the thralls of the land and the farmers, but we have nowhere near the luxury of the great halls of our nobility.'

Bartolo shrugged, implying that he'd heard all sorts of excuses over the years.

'You are a long way from home, are you not?'

'Very.' It was unusual for Alcuin to be so close-mouthed, and it made Galen glance up at his friend's face. It told him nothing, but then Alcuin was good at not letting his emotions show. 'Like you, we were sent on a mission for our masters.'

'What kind of mission were you on?' Carbo asked, looking at Bartolo.

'Our mistress wanted us to make contact with a certain Geoffroi of—'

'Geoffroi the Heretic?' Carbo roared. 'Why would you want to speak to him? He has caused nothing but trouble. He and his followers go into towns and murder and pillage everything of value.'

'To distribute to the poor.'

'Only if the poor swear loyalty to him and give all they own to his followers to be distributed amongst them.'

'It's a just system. They distributed goods according to need.'

'Hah! And Geoffroi has the greatest need, no doubt. I hear he has an entire harem of women.'

'Concubinage and fraternising with the devil are the Church's standard accusations against everyone they disapprove of. Don't you think that's strange? You should think for yourself once in a while.'

'But what if it is true? Why else would the church say those things about heretics? Besides, we have seen it with our own eyes. The wild behaviour of the cult brings shame upon us all.'

'I see you are still wedded to the church and no sense will penetrate your thick skull.'

Bartolo's dismissive attitude and his outrageous views astonished Galen. He was aware that he was less conformist than most monks, but Galen had never met anyone in such blatant opposition to the church who still called himself a Christian. Hatim had been critical of the church, but that was because of his own religion. Even so, he followed the code of his faith.

But this Bartolo and his silent companion were in open rebellion. It was terrifying. Especially because Galen had some sympathy with their position, if not their uncritical view of Geoffroi.

'At least my saviour will welcome me into heaven,' Carbo said. 'Which is more than can be said for you.'

Bartolo gave him a cynical smile.

'And let us hope God welcomes his son Geoffroi into heaven with open arms too, for he has already been martyred. The viscount and the bishop of Toulouse, along with several more influential men of the church and the local nobility, decided Geoffroi was getting too powerful. The viscount brought in his warriors to crush Geoffroi's followers and they took Geoffroi away for trial.

'They threw all sorts of scurrilous accusations at him, which resulted in his execution. By the time we arrived in Toulouse, all that was left of Geoffroi's glorious uprising was his head, and those of the leaders of his church, on spikes at the gate.'

'It's what he deserved,' Carbo said. 'We saw how he murdered half a town, carried off their women and killed many monks during his rampage.'

'On how we feel about Geoffroi the Martyr, we will have to differ,' Bartolo said, with emphasis on the martyr, and there was a gleam in his eye that Galen couldn't interpret.

Perhaps it was fanaticism, but he wasn't sure. The story about Geoffroi and his end, and the confrontation between Bartolo and Carbo, made him shudder.

'Are you alright?' Alcuin asked. 'Is it too cold?'

'I'm fine.'

Galen wished that Alcuin's comment hadn't drawn Bartolo's curious gaze. Fortunately, he lost interest at one glance. Galen was familiar with that. He'd been weighed and found worthless. In the past, that dismissal would have left him feeling inadequate. Today, it merely filled him with relief.

The next moment, Carbo's enormous bulk blocked his view of Bartolo. The usual fear of the man bubbled up, but he pushed it resolutely away. He was being unfair. Brother Carbo had never done him any harm. On the contrary, he went out of his way to be helpful.

At first this had made Galen even more uneasy, for he couldn't understand his motives. The only explanation that he'd been able to think of was that the man might be interested in him. But if he was, he'd also shown consideration. Carbo kept his distance and only did what was asked of him. But he'd also gone to great lengths to be helpful, especially in the valley.

Now that Galen knew why, part of what made him uncomfortable in Carbo's presence was removed. Although it reminded him of the whole sainthood question, which he was trying his best to ignore. It wasn't him doing the miracles, after all; it was God. Why he'd been chosen as the Lord's vehicle he couldn't understand, but for the first time he was grateful that he was. If not for that, Alcuin would be dead.

Then again, if not for the miracles, neither of them would have been put at risk on this dangerous journey. Galen sighed and shook his head. This was the route his internal debate always landed up taking. Lacking a resolution was exhausting. Maybe going to see the pope was the right thing to do after all.

Chapter 14

The rest of the day continued in uncomfortable silence after the disagreements between Brothers Bartolo and Carbo, which resulted in Carbo's ongoing prickly demeanour. Galen had hoped that, despite the added safety of moving in a group, the newcomers would be faster than them and leave them behind.

As it turned out, the attached peasants were also slow. One emaciated woman and her equally thin child were even slower than Galen. So the group remained together.

At least nobody grumbled at the pace. Galen was only thankful that it was all downhill and that finally they came to a long flat stretch on the approach to a small town at the mouth of the river that ran through the valley.

From a distance they'd been able to see a simple long harbour that stretched into the mouth of the narrow river, a cluster of buildings and a small church whose tower poked above the thatched roofs. Even at this distance, Galen could swear he could smell the incense-like aroma of the woodsmoke drifting up through the thatch. For him, it was the smell of civilisation.

A small fleet of fishing boats was making its way back to the harbour as the travellers arrived at the outskirts of the town.

'We will stay with the local priest,' Carbo said, turning to Brother Bartolo and his group. 'I doubt he will welcome you.'

Bartolo gave him a cynical smile.

'We wouldn't want to associate with the local church anyway. I'm sure we'll be more than comfortable at the harbour.'

He turned his back on Galen's party and his exhausted people followed him the few steps to the harbour, where the fishermen were bringing in their catches and tying up their boats for the night.

It had been a long walk and Galen had pushed himself, partly to not be the person holding everyone back, but also because he desperately wanted a quiet night in human habitation. All the same, he was so tired now that he stopped and leaned his head on his staff with a sigh.

'Are you alright?' Alcuin asked. 'You're hanging on the staff, using it to keep yourself upright. Do you need to sit down?'

Galen nodded tiredly, taking in the few local townsfolk who were eyeing them with curiosity but, perhaps because of their habits, no animosity.

'We're nearly there. Just give me a moment to catch my breath and then we can continue.'

'Just a short rest, then. After which you can lean on me and we can take it easy.'

'Or you can lean on me. I'll hardly feel it,' Carbo said.

'No,' Galen said, too quickly, and immediately regretted it.

'Why not?' Carbo fell to his knees before Galen and said, 'What have I done? Why am I so vile that you refuse to touch me?'

Galen was appalled for he hadn't realised how much he'd hurt Carbo, but he also couldn't stop himself and stepped back.

'Please,' Carbo said and reached out to clutch the hem of Galen's habit, 'please don't shun me!'

'I'm sorry,' Galen said, deeply mortified. 'I didn't realise I was hurting you.'

'I wasn't always a monk. I was an enforcer for a powerful warlord for many years and the things I did... they weren't good. But I've changed and I've repented. I swear.'

Galen looked about himself. A few of the townsfolk had stopped to stare at the spectacle of a great big monk grovelling at the feet of one who surely looked insignificant. One man was leaning in his doorway, a straw between his teeth, watching with as much interest as if Galen was a wandering gleeman.

'I know nothing of you and your life,' he said softly, thankful the locals probably couldn't understand Latin.

'So why do you shun me?'

'I was... I was attac—' Galen stopped and took a deep breath. He'd never voluntarily told this tale to anyone. But now he did owe Carbo an explanation. He knew what it was to be ostracised, and yet he'd inflicted the same pain on another. 'No... I was raped by a man who was big... big like you. To see you... brings back those memories... It makes me fear you.'

'Holy Mary, Mother of God, you were raped?!'

Galen flushed uncomfortably at the horror in Carbo's voice.

'I think that's why... that's why I sometimes heal others but can't do the same for myself. I... I am unclean.'

'No!' Alcuin murmured. 'It wasn't your fault.'

Galen gave a wry smile, shrugged, and tugged at Carbo to get the big man to stand up.

'Being attacked... it causes many scars,' Carbo said. 'I never raped anyone, be they man or woman, but I beat many to a pulp. And I... once came upon one of my former victims. I was already a monk by then, but it made no difference. He took one look at me and ran. He couldn't be anywhere near me. I have never felt more remorse than at that moment.'

Galen was trembling and he couldn't work out whether that was from tiredness or the emotion of this confession.

Carbo pushed himself up off his knees, nodding.

'I understand now. I won't do anything you don't want me to.'

'Thank you,' Galen said, looking up at the man who now towered over him. 'I will try... I will try to overcome my fear of you.'

'That would be good indeed.'

'Maybe...' Galen said, taking a deep breath because he was still shaken by the encounter, 'maybe you could lend me your arm.'

'Yes, I'll do that,' Carbo said, and his voice thickened with emotion.

Galen held out a trembling hand and Carbo took it from underneath and, with exaggerated care, slowly took Galen's weight.

Galen gave him a tight-lipped, hopefully not too apprehensive smile, his hand clenched around Carbo's enormous fist, and started back along the path. Carbo gave him an astonished look, but followed the lead and, keeping his arm crooked so that he took much of Galen's weight, fell into step with him.

If he hadn't been still so overwhelmed himself, Galen might have laughed now because Carbo was behaving much as any giant would who was suddenly given something of tremendous fragility into his care and was afraid he'd damage it. He was being extra careful as he walked beside Galen, watching his every move so that he could respond instantly to it.

'And so you win another person over,' Alcuin murmured into Galen's ear in Englisc. 'With your gesture of trust, I doubt there's anything Carbo won't do for you now. It's fortunate that you're not the kind of person who would use Carbo, knowing what power you have over him.'

The observation astonished Galen. He was less convinced that Carbo would be so easily manipulated. In his experience, it took force of will and physical power to get people to follow a man. But perhaps it made some sense of what he'd heard of Geoffroi the Heretic, who had gathered a following of hundreds.

'There it is - the church,' Carbo said of the biggest building in the village. 'Fra' Arnal told me that the priest there has often arranged passage for travellers from here to Rome, for he knows all the sailors.'

'That's good,' Alcuin said, examining the faces of the passersby.

It felt to Galen that they didn't look overly interested to see them. This was apparently a town which saw plenty of strangers come and go. As a result, they were less welcoming than in some villages they'd come upon where the people had been eager to meet travellers and have a chat.

'I'll go in search of the priest,' Carbo said. 'You wait here where Brother Galen can sit on this wall. I don't think he should walk another step. At least only as far as a bed, which I will also arrange for us.'

Galen watched Carbo go with such a look of surprise that Alcuin burst out laughing.

'What do you expect when you've been so good to him? You only have yourself to blame for his solicitude.'

'All I did was take his arm.'

'No, you explained, and then you took his arm. That took a great deal of courage.'

Galen shook his head, unwilling to discuss the matter further. Fortunately, Alcuin didn't push it. His consideration was such that he wouldn't do anything that tired Galen.

'At least we'll be on a ship for most of the rest of this journey,' Alcuin said. 'You've been more hunched up walking today. I think that fall did more harm than you've admitted to so far.'

Alcuin felt a prickle of embarrassment pass over him as Carbo came out of the church, hotly followed by an angular, bony, very expectant-looking priest. It seemed Carbo had told all, and part of the story was about Alcuin after all. Now he knew how Galen felt. Alcuin didn't want to hear talk of the incident either.

'This is Father Manleu. He says we're welcome to his house and his table for the night. He's also given me the name of a ship's captain. I'll go and have a chat with him about giving us a ride.'

'Goodness me, goodness me, yes,' Father Manleu said as Carbo headed off. 'Bless my soul! An actual saint come to visit my humble home in our little village. What will the people say when they hear this?'

'Ah,' Alcuin said as Galen's grip tightened on his arm. 'We would be grateful if you don't tell anybody about this. At least, not until we've left.'

'But good heavens, why? Surely a miracle is cause for rejoicing. We should praise God and thank Him for His mercy.'

Alcuin felt so tired that he didn't want this conversation.

'Perhaps later,' Galen said.

'But are you not the beneficiary of His miracle?' Father Manleu said.

His comment threw both Alcuin and Galen for a second.

'Ah,' Alcuin said. This wasn't the first time such a thing had happened. 'You think I'm the saint. But actually, it's Galen.'

The priest's eyes widened as he looked from Alcuin to Galen and back to Alcuin.

'He's the saint?'

'Well, at least, that's for the pope to decide,' Alcuin said. 'Which is why we are not saying anything to people yet.'

'I see, I see,' Father Manleu said, while rubbing his stubbly chin. 'Well, well, so that's how it is, mmm? You'd better come in then.'

He led Alcuin and Galen into a small house with a low-roofed, single room with a fire in the middle, a simple table and bench on the left, and a bed on the other side of the fire against the right wall.

'Shoo!'

Father Manleu flapped his hands at a cat who had a paw hooked in under the cloth that covered a pile of jars and plates in the middle of the table. The cat hopped off the table and sauntered out of the house.

'Such a nuisance,' Father Manleu said, but without heat. 'Please, sit down. You've come a long way and have even further to go.'

Then he pulled away the cloth like one revealing treasure. It was certainly a sight that pleased Alcuin as he helped Galen sit on the bench. Before them was a wooden board holding a plump, pale yellow cheese, a pot of honey, a plate with bacon, another with a grilled fish, the stick still steaming as it poked through the body, and half a loaf of bread. Alcuin grinned at Galen, who only gave him a distracted smile. He seemed to be mesmerised by the priest, who kept up a stream of conversation with no response needed from his audience.

'Here, have some wine,' Father Manleu said as he poured from a full terracotta jug into a trio of mugs and hastily filled a fourth one for Carbo, whose arrival shrank the room. He was so big it felt there was no space left in the house. Carbo took the offered wine with a delighted grin. He sat on the edge of the bed, took a large gulp that Alcuin assumed emptied the mug, and wiped the back of his hand across his mouth in satisfaction.

'I've found us a boat to Genua. We'll easily be able to find another ship from there on to Rome. Genua is a much bigger port than this little place. The condition of passage is that we help load and unload the boat. I said you and I can do that, Brother Alcuin, but Brother Galen won't. I told them they'd do well to take us though, because it can only bring good fortune to carry a saint on their ship.'

Galen choked on his wine and sent a fine spray across the table.

'You shouldn't have told them that. The last time we took a ship, we were shipwrecked!'

'But you survived. How many people actually survive a shipwreck?' Carbo said with a logic Alcuin couldn't refute.

Galen shook his head.

'You shouldn't go about saying anything about saints, Carbo. It isn't wise, and it isn't true.'

'How can you say that when I saw you perform a miracle with my own eyes?'

Galen flushed and said, 'You should at least wait till we've been to Rome and had someone in authority tell us whether or not we're right.'

'But it's true. How can it not be? Brother Alcuin would have died if—'

'Peace, Galen's tired. Let's not have an argument tonight,' Alcuin said as he held up his hand.

'No, of course,' Carbo said with a quick, apologetic bow. 'I was forgetting myself.'

'All the same,' Father Manleu said, 'there are plenty of people who make a big show of performing miracles. Geoffroi the Heretic claimed he could double the food his followers foraged.'

'Did he really do that?'

It was typical Galen, Alcuin thought, to ask about a false saint in the same spirit of enquiry as he asked about the saints they discussed in the chapter house.

'Of course he didn't,' Father Manleu said with a laugh. 'His rabble passed through our village too. They plundered our stores and killed a few of the men who tried to stop them. This was before they headed to Toulouse and he met his deserved end. A hungrier, more ragged bunch I have never seen before.

'If he could double their food, he wasn't doing a good job. But it's a sign of the times. His might have been the biggest band to have come through, but they aren't the only band. He was a smooth talker, though. He even convinced a handful of my flock to join him. Much good it did them.'

'So you heard he was dealt with, then?' Carbo asked.

'Two of the villagers came crawling back with their tails between their legs and told us all about it. The rest died when the viscount's men swooped in, trapping the lot of them like rats, and hacked them to pieces. This was after the trial, when his followers tried to break him out of the prison. More fool them.'

Carbo tutted in agreement as the priest handed him a slice of bread with a large wedge of cheese on top.

'We came across such a group ourselves. They are currently camped on the docks by the boats.'

'Ah, the people won't like that. I dare say the fishermen will either drive them off or stay up all night guarding their boats. They're less welcoming than they were before these riffraff started appearing.'

'There are two monks leading this group.'

'They're the worst. They're better educated than the rabble they attract and better able to convince them of their cause. To see the corruption of the clergy like this breaks my heart.'

Alcuin watched Galen absorbing the conversation, indecipherable thoughts flickering across his face. Alcuin would have loved to know what Galen really thought of the situation, but he knew his friend wouldn't say anything before these strangers. Sometimes he suspected Galen didn't divulge all his thoughts, even when it was just the two of them. Still, he was curious to know what his clever friend made of these uprisings.

Chapter 15

'We are not going on the same boat as them!' Brother Carbo said when they arrived at the harbour at dawn to find Brothers Bartolo and Gentile and their little group already loading the waiting ship.

It did not surprise Galen to see them, as they were heading in the same direction. He was also curious to learn more about them, but, at the same time, filled with trepidation. The last thing he and Alcuin needed was to be pulled into anything that endangered their mission.

For both their sakes, he wanted to get to Rome as quickly as possible so that they could go home. He worried nonstop about his family and what might be happening to them. He also wondered whether these wandering bands of cultists had sprung up in Engla-lond.

'There are no other boats,' Brother Bartolo said in a tone bordering on the insolent.

It seemed he actively worked on riling Brother Carbo. Or perhaps that was just his nature and why he'd ended up outside the church rather than in it. A man who was always poking and provoking could expect to be thrown out, or worse, before long.

At least he was a hard worker and didn't even pause in the business of loading the heavy-looking, blue stained sacks they'd be sharing the deck with. Galen was watching the activity along with the scrawny woman and child, the only ones exempted from loading the ship. The woman had given Galen an awkward smile, bobbing to him in greeting, but as neither spoke the other's tongue, they could go no further than that.

'That's woad,' Father Manleu said.

He'd also taken up a position beside Galen, who wasn't surprised that the priest had accompanied them to the harbour. Their little group provided the man with more entertainment than he'd had in a while. Galen was grateful he'd kept quiet about the miracle so far, but was certain that the moment they left, tales of saints and miracles would fly through the village.

'The dye?' Galen said as he realised the priest was waiting.

'It's what we're famous for around here. The blue dye from our county is the best in the world.'

'I see,' Galen said and fell back into introspection.

He was never very good at small talk. Fortunately, the priest didn't mind and waxed lyrical about all the wonders of his home and its surroundings. Galen supposed it was human nature to have pride in the place you were born, as if it showed some inherent wisdom of your own for having landed up in it. Galen was less impressed.

This County of Toulouse didn't compare favourably with home. They had more land at their disposal, yet they didn't appear to prosper from it. Their nobility seemed to treat their people more harshly too. Galen had no illusions that people had a hard time in Engla-lond, but it looked worse here.

It made him wonder what conditions were like for the average people of Al-Andalus. He'd never been able to leave the palace there, but the city that had surrounded it appeared to be better organised and more prosperous than anywhere else he'd ever been. That brought a wry smile to his lips. Who'd have thought that he'd wind up seeing more of the world than his warrior brothers? They sometimes travelled around Engla-lond, accompanying the king, but they'd never left their island.

'Are you ready?' Alcuin asked while dusting his hands that had also gained a blue cast.

'I am. I hope those sacks weren't too heavy,' Galen said as he glanced across at the woman and child.

The two looked anxious about the journey. Even so, she hurried past Galen and Alcuin and up onto the ship. Brother Carbo was still standing on the dock and offered Galen a hand up onto the ramp that heaved up and down between the boat and the platform.

Just seeing that motion made Alcuin's face blanch and gave Galen a pang of guilt. There really wasn't a faster route to Rome and this way they'd bypass the unimaginably high Alps. So, despite feeling bad for his friend, he allowed Carbo to heave him onto the ship and guide him, with exaggerated care, to a space amongst the cargo just large enough for three and as far away from Bartolo and Gentile and their group as could be managed on a ship.

'You're keeping us apart,' Galen murmured.

'It's better this way.'

Galen was sure he was right as he settled on a lumpy sack and scooted along so that Alcuin could sit next to him. He was looking forward to the speed and the comfort of the voyage, which meant he could sit still and look around. It was a sunny morning and the choppy waves dazzled as they reflected the bright light.

'The ship's captain says it will only take two or three days to get to Genua. He says the only thing to pray against are pirates and autumn showers.'

Alcuin shuddered, and Galen couldn't tell if that was from fear or nausea. Then he groaned and, as the ship cast off, Alcuin heaved himself up the side of the boat and threw up. Galen had been expecting it but was still dismayed that it had happened so quickly. It was why he'd asked Carbo to arrange more than the usual amount of wine for their onward journey.

He'd have preferred beer, but the local beverage of choice seemed to be wine, especially at this time of the year when the grapes had just been harvested and wine was plentiful. Alcuin might not be able to keep his food down, but Galen had learned when they crossed the Channel that it was essential to drink as much as an ailing man could to keep up his strength. He was therefore determined to make Alcuin drink as much wine as he could get down the man's throat. No matter how much he resisted.

In the meantime, he had little else to do but watch the scenery drift by and listen to the chatter of the sailors. They, according to Carbo, were all Franks, so Galen couldn't understand a word. But he found the language interestingly musical.

The rest of the time he spent observing Brother Bartolo's party. The two monks might say they were in sympathy with the common man, but Galen had his doubts. Brother Gentile was harder to read and, as he didn't speak, it was understandable that he had no communication with the followers. Although on occasion Galen had seen him using hand gestures with Brother Bartolo.

The younger monk, or ex-monk, also ignored the people, only talking to them when they made requests of him. Even then, he looked irritated to be bothered and usually just sent them away. Whether he gave them useful advice, Galen couldn't tell because he, too, was speaking Frankish.

Alcuin was relieved that the waves of the Mediterranean were milder than on the sea off Engla-Lond. He still threw up though, and spent most of the journey hunched miserably over the edge of the boat, trying to control his revolting stomach.

Galen sat beside him, his hand resting on his shoulder, but not saying anything. Alcuin was thankful for both signs of sympathy. He was even more pleased when the boat finally sailed into Genua harbour.

'Look at that!' Galen said and his eyes were as wide as cart wheels. 'This harbour is huge and round. See that Alcuin?'

'I see it. Although I'd prefer to be looking at it from the comfort of those very solid-looking harbour walls.'

'Their harbour is made of stone too.'

'So it is. Truly, these people are remarkable. They use stone even when there is plenty of wood around.'

'Stone must surely last longer.'

'I suppose so, but imagine the effort required to put it in place.'

Galen nodded as his eyes drifted out across the harbour, taking in the impressive stone walls that formed its foundation.

'Don't worry, we'll soon be there. And then you can have a proper meal and a proper sleep.'

Alcuin groaned.

'I forbid you to talk about food until we're sitting on something that doesn't constantly heave up and down.'

'You have my word. And look, Carbo's helping with the sails. He's really enjoyed this trip too.'

'Good, I'm glad. Does this mean you've had a good time?'

'I have. I've just sat still beside you whilst Carbo's organised everything. It is quite an astonishing place. So many mountains, such big ones too, and they come right up to the edge of the sea. And everything is bright and harsh. The land is almost reduced to dust with no covering of grass where they haven't had rain, and the trees are darker here than at home, like they've been burned by the sun.'

'Maybe they have. I suddenly feel like I should have been paying attention so that I could draw all you have described.'

'There's still plenty of time. We're only halfway to Rome, apparently.'

'Oh God, have mercy!' Alcuin murmured. 'You mean I still have more of this hell to get through?'

'You knew we still had to go on from Genua!'

'I didn't realise this was only a halfway mark. I pray Carbo doesn't find it so easy to find us a ship to Rome. A couple of days on shore would do me good.'

Unfortunately, Alcuin wasn't to have his wish. Within hours of walking ashore, the three monks were once again loading a ship and heading out to sea.

'There is no fairness to this life,' Alcuin muttered as he curled up in a miserable bundle.

'At least this time we are on our own,' Carbo said. 'We no longer have the company of the heretics.'

This was true. The last Alcuin saw of Brothers Bartolo and Gentile and their little group was Bartolo giving a dismissive salute as they sailed away. Alcuin was relieved to see the back of them too. Galen's interest in them made him uneasy. Honestly, Galen's curiosity was going to get them into trouble one day. Instead of seeing the enemy for what they were and condemning them, he was fascinated. It had been the same in Al-Andalus where Galen had been far too interested in and open-minded about the culture.

The boat wallowed from side to side, which was always the worst. Alcuin's stomach lurched with it and he hastily pressed his hand to his mouth.

'Distract me,' he said, casting a pleading gaze at Galen.

His friend looked immediately alarmed for his health, which left Alcuin feeling guilty.

'Should I describe the scenery?'

Alcuin raised his gaze from where he had it fixed on the sun-bleached planks of the boat to peep over the side. The rocky and mountainous land beyond seemed to heave along with the sea.

'Dear God, no,' Alcuin said, hastily looking back at the deck. 'Something else. Test me with one of your riddles.'

'A riddle?'

Galen was quiet for so long that Alcuin flicked a look up to his face that was twitching as he apparently considered one riddle after another.

'Quickly!'

'Alright, here's one,' Galen said:

'Earth-fast it stands, this object I know
Deaf and dumb, it daily swallows
From thrall's hands, useful gifts
From the town the thane, solemn and swarthy
Into its mouth, sends more of these
Desired by princes, dearer than gold
Kings and queens, now and forever
Never name its nature, those who profit from it
The dauntless and gallant, take all that dumb thing
That witless dull faced dunce, eagerly swallows.'

'I see you didn't spare me in complexity,' Alcuin said. 'It's a good one.'

'So you haven't figured it out?'

'There wasn't much chance of working it out immediately,' Alcuin said, concentrating ferociously on the puzzle so that he couldn't think about anything else. 'It's going to take a while. Repeat it for me.'

Galen obeyed, reciting the riddle slower.

'That is tough,' Alcuin said.

'How do you normally solve puzzles?'

'What a funny question. I... conjure up an image of each line and see where it leads me. In this instance, an object that stands firm on the ground and swallows up all that is brought to it. Things of great value like gems and golden torques. Maybe it's a treasure chest.'

'Perhaps,' Galen murmured and repeated the riddle once again.

'Ha, the first and most obvious solution is never the right one, is it?' Alcuin said. 'But it often provides clues as to what the object might actually be. How do you solve riddles?'

'I focus on the words themselves and see what deeper meaning each might have. I rarely have an image in my mind.'

'How fascinating,' Alcuin said and swallowed hard as the boat rocked even more violently. 'For you it's the words and for me it's the images. But perhaps there is a clue in that. After all, the treasure in the riddle is said to be dearer than gold.'

'That is true.'

Perhaps it was his seasickness that made it hard to concentrate, or merely the wish to be distracted, but Alcuin puzzled over the riddle for a good few hours, tossing out ideas that Galen just shook his head at, before the solution finally came to him.

'Might it perhaps be a bookcase?'

'I knew you'd get it in the end,' Galen said with a laugh. 'You're good with riddles.'

'Not as good as you.'

'Would you like another?'

'Later. For now I'm going to close my eyes and give myself up to misery,' Alcuin said, and he rolled himself into a ball and covered his head with his cloak.

Chapter 16

'This is surely not Rome,' Galen said, looking about.

They'd disembarked in the early morning in a not very sizeable harbour on a wide marshland where, despite the lateness of the season, black clouds of insects hung in the air over the rank reeds and grass. The harbour was at least full of boats, and the land humming with people, some shouting about their wares from the stalls that lined the harbour, some shopping, and others loading goods onto wagons and pack mules or a row of barges moored along a riverbank. Despite all this noise and activity, it felt rather makeshift and definitely not like a city.

'I see no hills. Isn't Rome built upon seven hills? This isn't the glory I was expecting.'

'This isn't Rome. For that we need to head inland.' Carbo hoisted his sack and slipped the strap over his head. 'But first we should stop at a stall and buy some food. We're nearly out of money, but we should have enough to keep us fed till we reach Rome.'

'I don't understand,' Alcuin said. 'I thought it was here too.'

'No, it's a couple of days' walk up the Tiberis River. The river is too shallow for the cargo boats to navigate, so barges and carts take the produce to and from this harbour. I'm afraid I couldn't find a barge willing to take us upriver for free.'

'That's alright,' Galen said, because he was feeling well rested and relatively pain free. 'I'm sure the walk won't be that difficult and Alcuin can use a break from boats.'

'I know the river is a lot less choppy than the sea, but I'll be glad if we walk,' Alcuin said. 'It will give me a chance to get back to my old self before we arrive at the Holy See and try to gain an audience with the pope.'

'You are going to see the pope himself, are you?'

'I hope so. Bishop Sigburt had a letter summoning him to Rome. So the pope will want to know why Sigburt hasn't come. I only hope I get to deliver that message myself and not via an intermediary.'

'Well, I shouldn't think it will be easy,' Carbo said, as he guided Alcuin and Galen to the market, surging through the chattering crowds who fell away to let the big man pass.

Galen was inclined to agree. Just getting to see his own father, a mere ealdorman, would have been next to impossible for most people. How much harder to see the pope? But at least they had to try. Failing that, they'd have to come up with another idea.

Most of the time, Galen tried not to think about miracles, but Alcuin and Bishop Sigburt's confidence in the pope's final say on the matter had made Galen start to believe in it too. So, one way or the other, he was determined to complete this undertaking. In the meantime, there was much to be seen and absorbed, starting with the shops. They had approached a baker and the smell of his fresh bread made Galen's mouth water. Even Carbo couldn't understand the locals, but that wasn't really necessary with food when he could point and hold his fingers up for a quantity.

He bought them a loaf of bread and a flagon of wine along with three skewers of squid grilled over hot coals.

'That's delicious,' Galen said as they set off on the main road that would finally get them to Rome. 'I don't think I've ever had something like this. It's better than grilled oysters.'

Alcuin pulled a face and muttered, 'I don't like these squishy legs. Give me oysters anytime over this.'

Galen grinned at him. He'd come to realise that while Alcuin loved to see new things and draw them, that was where his curiosity ended. When it came to food or different experiences, he got a bit grumpy.

Carbo laughed and said, 'But Brother Alcuin, the legs are the best part!'

Walking and eating, the trio made it out of the harbour town. They were surrounded by pedestrians, carts and mule trains as Galen expected of a major route leading to one of the most important cities in the world. The passing merchants occasionally tried to set up a conversation and Carbo always replied back. Realising they couldn't understand each other, the merchants grinned, flapping their hands in apology, and turned to others for their entertainment.

The path they were on was a relief for Galen because it was made from broad flat stones. They were a bit uneven but it was still easier than the unpaved mountain tracks they'd followed up till now. The road was also quite straight and flat and it was easy to see where they were headed.

After a couple of hours of walking, the marshland started to be dotted with firmer patches of land where trees had taken root. They looked like little islands amongst the flowing grass. Finally there was more solid ground than marsh around them and in the distance there appeared to be a ruined town.

'What's that?'

'Oh that. It's Ostia,' Carbo said, waving his hand as if to say it was of no interest.

But as they got closer, Galen could see that the town must have been of great importance, for the buildings were large, although now sunk halfway or more into the black soil.

'This must have been an important place,' Alcuin said, running his hand up and down a massive white square block with the look of the top of what must once have been a mighty gate, of which only the uppermost part remained visible.

'Did it sink?' Galen asked.

'It silted up.' Carbo barely glanced at the stone. 'This used to be the main harbour of Rome when the Roman Empire was at its height. But because of the silt from the river, the harbour has gradually moved westward.'

'How do you know these things?' Galen asked.

'Because I've been to Rome before. This is my third time and you learn things when you travel.'

Carbo spoke gloomily, as if learning was something to be avoided. Galen had come across this attitude before. His father had once said that ignorance kept people in their place and made them easier to rule, but even so he wasn't for that.

Galen ran his fingers along the smooth carved relief of the stone rump of a horse. It was one of a dozen similar horses, all mounted by well armed and armoured Roman soldiers. Behind these figures were ranks of legionaries heading out into battle.

'It's that same white stone the Moors use.'

'Marble,' Alcuin said. 'But here it's carved with scenes of the Roman army and, I assume, the battle it commemorates. Whereas the Moorish-sculpted and decorated walls had no images of people or animals.'

'No, they didn't, did they? I didn't notice that.'

'You were ill and then you were distracted.'

'But you noticed, and that is how it should be, for you are an artist.'

Carbo's eyes swept uninterestedly over the carving. He was like the other travellers who probably used the path so frequently they'd ceased to notice things that were wonderful to Galen and Alcuin. The traffic didn't even slow and the only other people who approached the ruins were a man who used a wall to shield himself from view as he took a pee, and a pair of children who darted about the ruins playing hide and seek before their mother called them back to her.

'It's ancient history and no use to us,' Carbo said. 'It would be better to break up this godless monument and use the stone for something useful, like a church.'

'Oh no!' Galen was surprised that anyone would want to tear down a thing of beauty, even if pagans put it up. 'The Romans were a mighty race. We should have reminders of them and the glory men can attain.'

'People don't need that kind of reminder. They're already trying to live idle lives. It's the wrong way. They should aim to lead better lives so that they gain their reward in heaven, not here on Earth.'

'What's wrong with having a comfortable life on Earth?' Galen asked, taken aback by the heat in Carbo's voice.

This was also a familiar attitude. There were many people in the church, the founder of his order, Saint Benedict, included, that believed in a simple way of life. Galen was all for simplicity. But he didn't understand why it had to be taken to the extremes of poverty and discomfort.

'Lusting after comfort leads to the deadly sins of sloth, envy and gluttony and can only lead to strife because not everybody has it or can ever have it,' Carbo said. 'There are far too many people for all the world's goods to be shared equally. Look around you, see how many people are poor and suffering.

'I myself come from a large family. My mother bore twenty-six children but only five of us grew to adulthood, and even that was a struggle. The temptation to turn to crime was great. But it was when I realised I had to look after my soul and make sure I earned my place in heaven that I finally found peace.'

Galen squinted up at Carbo, trying to understand the big man and find an argument he could put in return. Questions of fairness and equality had often preoccupied him. Because of this, he'd considered the structure of society and how it all fitted together.

He understood the need for strong men like his father. They could protect the people from danger, be that bands of robbers or raiding Vikings. Hugh also ensured the peaceful and fair administration of his land. His fellow ealdormen did the same. All of them, in turn, deferred to the king.

The thralls and churls provided the food and additional men in times of war. The men and women of the soil were far too busy and too weak to get involved in administration or defence. So, even with some unfairness, or the existence of cruel lords, the system worked and benefitted everyone.

It was also because of that system that holy orders could exist. They needed stability to manage the administration of legal documents, as well as praying for the safety of their kingdom. Each group depended upon the other, and no part could survive without the other.

They couldn't all wall themselves off in little monasteries, as Carbo had done. But Galen said none of this. Awestruck as the big monk appeared to be about meeting a possible saint, Galen doubted he could shift his deep-seated beliefs.

Besides, there was so much to see that he didn't want to waste time in an argument because now, to their left, was an unusual hexagonal-shaped lake.

'Trajan's port,' Carbo said in reply to Galen's questioning look. 'It's where the boats used to dock.'

'It's impressive even now,' Galen said as the road they were on, that kept the Tiberis River to their right, widened, the paving improved markedly, and it became straight as a rule. 'Look at this road, Alcuin. Just like the Roman roads in Engla-lond.'

'Except wider,' Alcuin said as they left the ghost town of Ostia and were back into the countryside.

The roads here were lined with a kind of pine that Galen didn't recognise. Pine trees were rare at home, but those he'd seen were scraggy, tall, thin and tapered towards the top. These were quite different, with no lower branches but a lush green canopy that appeared bulbous in the younger-looking trees but flattened out to a curving canopy in the taller, older trees.

As they made their way along the path, the land rose about them, till they were walking on the flat ground the Tiberis had carved through a ridge that ran parallel to the sea. On the heights were clusters of these same pines that looked like fluffy green clouds.

'Such a vivid green,' Alcuin murmured, following Galen's gaze, 'against an equally vivid blue. It's beautiful. I don't think I've ever seen light like it.'

'It's different, isn't it? The light feels autumnal, like at home, but brighter and clearer. I wonder what those trees are called. I suspect they've been planted for more than just their beauty.'

'They're umbrella pines,' Carbo said. 'They produce an edible nut.'

'A nut? From a pine tree? How is that possible?' Alcuin said.

'They're not very big.' Carbo held his thumb and forefinger up as if holding an invisible nut the size of a grain of wheat. 'You'll get to try it in Rome. The locals love the stuff.'

'But you don't?' Galen asked.

'It tastes a bit like resin so I'm not over fond of it, although they are better once they've been toasted. Either way, we need to hurry or it will be night before we reach Rome.'

Galen nodded and tried to walk faster while still looking around. But, rested as he was, any attempt at speed brought pain with it. And he was approaching the point where he'd need to rely on more than the support from his staff. Alcuin noted this and slowed right down in that way he had, as if it was the pace he wished to set for himself.

Galen gave him a grateful smile then went back to looking around. Across the valley and up the sides of the hills were the beginnings of farmland with rows of olive trees, lines of grapevines and the occasional field where the crops had already been harvested. Summers were very different here. Even the long grass left for grazing had turned brown and only now, after the autumn rains had begun, did a few shoots of fresh green grass peep out of the soil. This was such a rarity to Galen that he could count on the fingers of one hand the number of times the lack of rain had turned fields brown in Engla-lond.

The riverbank side of the path was greener. Heavily pruned willows, that were little more than bulbous club-like trunks, and tall reeds frequently obstructed views of the river where the occasional barge drifted past. One bargeman had struck up a song and his voice drifted across to them long after he himself had vanished from view.

The bargemen seemed to be particularly noisy, as another two were having a loud altercation. Galen assumed it was due to a near collision, but he couldn't understand what the men were saying. Some words were vaguely familiar, but not close enough to understand what the argument was about.

'I thought they'd all speak Latin.'

'It's the veritable Tower of Babel around here,' Carbo said. 'There are thousands of local dialects.'

'I see.'

Galen knew the world was teeming with dialects. It had even taken him a while to get used to the accents and dialects of his own people when he'd arrived in Yarmwick. But at least they'd all had Latin to fall back upon. Galen doubted the local people here would understand his Latin. It seemed he and Alcuin would have to rely upon translators, or remain within the religious community.

Chapter 17

Galen wiped his brow with the sleeve of his habit to stop the sweat from filtering through his eyebrows and slipping into his eyes.

'It's remarkably hot for late autumn, isn't it?' Alcuin said.

Galen nodded, noting that Alcuin's face, which had tanned during their journey, was also shiny with perspiration.

'They don't really say much about the weather in the lives of the saints that we've read and discussed at home, do they? I'm amazed at how different everything is. I remember tales of high adventure in my father's hall that led me to understand things were different far away. But they spoke of wonders such as elephants that are creatures the size of a house and monsters of the deep too horrible even to describe. I just assumed the kingdoms nearer us would be more similar.'

'Although the Frankish monks who came to visit Yarmwick did complain about the cold and the damp in our summer,' Alcuin said. 'As I recall, they said their summers were warmer and their winters brighter but colder.'

'That is true,' Galen said and tried to recall everything he'd heard about Rome.

The approaching sound of drums broke his concentration, and as he turned to look back, he also made out the high, reedy tone of a wind instrument and the clapping of hands.

'Well, I'll be!' Alcuin said as he came to a stop and also looked around. 'It's a band of travelling entertainers.'

'I wouldn't be so sure of that.' Carbo's voice was heavy with disapproval. 'Best just stand aside and let them go on their way.'

'What are they?' Galen asked. 'Are they a cult?'

'I expect so. That Bartolo fellow said he was heading for Rome, didn't he? I wouldn't be surprised if he was in this crowd, stirring up trouble.'

'They don't look troublesome. Everybody's smiling.'

'Don't you trust it, or any of them, Brother Galen. They're best avoided.'

Avoidance wasn't an option though, as the band was big. Galen guessed there must be at least a hundred men, women and children in the group. As they walked past, banging on drums and blowing on whistles, he felt increasingly intimidated and drew back, interposing Carbo's enormous bulk between him and this rowdy crowd. All the same, they fascinated him and he took the time, while he waited for them to pass, to scrutinise them.

They looked happy, but it had an edge to it. It felt like excitement mingled with a tingling dread. A lot of them were thin and most were badly dressed. Their clothes were threadbare rags, and many of them went barefoot. Galen also noticed a couple of men dressed as priests in the gathering, who seemed to be marshalling the group and trying to impose order. If he hadn't met Bartolo and Gentile earlier on, the priests might have come as more of a surprise. But not anymore.

Finally, there were only a few stragglers bringing up the rear. But at the end of this excitable gathering walked a woman who drew the eye for the serenity that clung to her. She smiled as she walked, nodding to things the people were pointing out and laughing as children detached themselves from their parents, dashed to her with some important confidence and then ran back to their mothers.

Although her clothes were sun bleached, they were of good quality and not patched. She wore a simple pale tan dress with a slightly darker tan robe over the top. Her hair was white and done up in a plait that hung over her shoulder and nearly brushed the ground.

'Now who have we here?' the woman said as she came to a stop before Galen's group.

She spoke perfect Latin in a warm, rich voice. Galen stopped breathing. Up close, her eyes were blue as the sky, clear and calm. She had a serenity he'd never seen before. She was also the same age as his mother, which caused a physical pain in Galen's heart.

'You need not concern yourself with us,' Carbo said.

'Is that so?' the woman said, and a gentle smile touched her lips. 'You have no need to fear us, big man. We are merely on a pilgrimage to Rome.'

'And what will you do when you get there?'

'We will seek an audience with the pope. I will ask him to do something for my followers. Each person you see here has suffered, just as the three of you have suffered. We will ask the pope whether he believes that is fair and we will ask him to do something about it.'

'Something like what?'

'Like distributing some of the vast wealth the church has amassed, to help its people.'

'I knew it! You want a handout. Well, let me tell you, you won't get one. What's more, you don't deserve one. Everyone must work as God intended. Then the earth will be bountiful for them.'

'Is that what you believe? Ah, my son, you are mistaken. Amongst the people who follow me are some of the hardest workers on the Earth. Yet rains fail, crops become blighted, plague stalks the land and lords make unreasonable demands which have driven these people out onto the roads in search of succour.'

'That happens to many people.'

'Indeed, it does, which is why we are going to Rome to ask the pope to intercede. We want his help not only for us but for everyone who finds themselves in the same tragic situation. Will you not join us on our pilgrimage?'

'No,' Carbo said flatly.

The woman smiled, and her eyes drifted over the three of them. She appeared entirely unconcerned by Carbo's animosity. And, Galen thought, she looked saintly. It made him want to step forward and touch her.

'Leave them be, Sister Marozia,' Bartolo said, surprising Galen as he emerged from the crowd that had stopped to see what was happening. 'They are too set in their ways to understand what you are trying to do.'

'No, Bartolo, there is goodness in them. I can see that. This big monk has lived a hard life, but he has repented. The beautiful young man next to him, watching us so expressionlessly, has lost a great love, and this quiet young man,' Marozia said, stepping up to Galen, 'well, he has suffered more than most. Haven't you, my son?'

Galen's heartbeat quickened to be singled out, and he took an involuntary step back.

'How do you know?'

'I know many things,' Marozia said and cupped her hand around the side of Galen's face. 'Oh child, how you long for a comforting embrace.'

'No,' Galen said jerkily, and Alcuin stepped between the two of them.

'He's a monk. You may not touch him.'

'My heart bleeds to know it is so,' Marozia said softly, removing her hand. 'For I would like nothing better than to lay my hands on him and heal the pain in his body and in his heart.'

'You'll do no such thing,' Carbo said. 'He doesn't need your help.'

'You don't know what you are talking about,' Bartolo snapped. 'Marozia has performed many miracles.'

'She... she has?' Galen asked and, despite himself, felt a spark of hope.

'That interests you,' Marozia said with her gentle smile. 'Come, walk with us and this evening you and I can have a talk about miracles.'

'We shouldn't,' Carbo said, looking imploringly at Galen.

'What harm can it do?'

Galen's question was sincere, even if it might be misinterpreted. Besides, much as Marozia and her band of followers intimidated Galen, he also wondered whether he might not get some answers from them.

'No harm at all, my dear. But if it makes your big brother feel more comfortable, we will leave you to follow in our wake or join us. Whichever you see fit.'

Marozia gave a slight conspiratorial smile and resumed her leisurely stroll. Bartolo gave Carbo a particularly annoyed look before following her, whispering something in her ear.

'I really don't like this,' Carbo said.

'Why not?'

Galen took the big man's arm, partly for support, for the pain had grown so much in his gut that walking had become difficult, but also to draw some courage from him as they fell into step a hundred yards or so behind Marozia.

'I don't trust that woman or her followers.'

'He has a point, Galen,' Alcuin said as he walked beside them, his eyes fixed on the rag-tag bunch.

'Why?'

'They are unruly. It isn't the harmonious group Marozia made it out to be. Look, even now her followers are stealing from the locals.' Alcuin pointed at a trio of boys who had scaled a large pear tree and were throwing the fruits down to the people below. 'They also argue amongst themselves and there's a couple of strong-looking men spread amongst the crowd to enforce order. I think Bartolo is one of them and he's none too gentle. Just now I saw him push another man and we haven't been following them for long.'

'But what of the things she spoke about, Alcuin? The miracles she performs and the fact that she knew so much about us.'

'That! They were good guesses. Anyone can tell from the scars on his face that Carbo has led a hard life. Anyone looking at my glorious image can guess that I've had romantic attachments. And I'm afraid, my friend, that being pale and bent over like you are, nobody would have any difficulty in guessing that you have suffered and continue to suffer.'

'And what about the rest?'

Galen was reluctant to give in to Alcuin's reasoning, sound as it was.

'The embrace? Who doesn't long for an embrace, Galen my friend? Especially when they are in pain.'

'Are you saying she's a fraud?'

'Maybe not that. Maybe she truly believes that she'll be able to see the pope and convince him, just as she has convinced so many to follow her.'

CHAPTER 18

Owing to the ease of following the road, Marozia's group continued walking until well into the night. It was reaching the point where Alcuin was going to insist that he and Galen stop because his friend's face had grown pale and drawn when Marozia called a halt beside a stand of tall poplar trees. Her followers fanned out into the fields to find somewhere to spend the night and campfires sprang up all around the three monks.

'About time,' Carbo said and unslung his bag right on the side of the road. He clearly had no intention of camping in somebody else's field. 'You need to rest, Brother Galen. We've walked long past when we normally stop.'

'I'm alright,' Galen said with a slight smile directed at both Carbo and Alcuin.

Alcuin had settled on a stone waymarker and suppressed his irritation that Carbo was usurping his position of managing Galen. There was no need for jealousy, after all.

'I still don't see why we've followed that rabble and didn't stop hours ago,' Carbo said. 'We could have easily parted company that way.'

'I want to stay with them,' Galen said.

'But why? They're nothing but trouble!'

'I want to talk to Marozia.'

'Just be wary of her.' Alcuin opened his bag and dug around, looking for Galen's tea. He'd be needing it after such a long walk. 'Don't let her draw you in.'

'I won't.'

'The problem is, you're too trusting. I'm worried about what might happen if she takes you in and then betrays you later on.'

'I'll try and be careful,' Galen said, although he flushed and his gaze dropped to the ground.

'I'm sorry, I shouldn't have said that,' Alcuin said and gave Galen's arm a reassuring squeeze. 'I just worry for you because Marozia offers the possibility of a miracle. It's enough to raise hopes in any breast.'

Galen nodded but still couldn't look Alcuin in the eye, so he knew he'd accurately read the reason for Galen wishing to stay near Marozia. He wondered whether Marozia would seek them out or would leave them alone now that they'd nominally joined her followers. He hoped she wouldn't turn up and, most of all, that she wouldn't attract Galen.

It wasn't very much later when Alcuin's hopes were dashed as he spotted Marozia working her way between her followers. She stopped now and then for a brief chat, but she was obviously making her way towards the monks. Not only that, but Galen had noticed her approach and was clasping his hands anxiously together, waiting.

'I see you are keeping yourselves apart,' Marozia said as she arrived.

'I won't join that rabble,' Carbo said.

'They are good people, like those who brought you up, and have merely fallen upon hard times.'

'And who are now stealing from those they pass.'

'We try to only take from those who have a little to spare.'

'How can you tell what they have to spare?'

'Have you not noticed that the field we are camped in has a large house attached to it? This is no peasant lodging. This is the land of a wealthy man.'

'It's still stealing and he would be within his rights to string up the lot of you.'

'He won't.'

'How can you be so sure?'

'Because God is looking after me and mine,' Marozia said with a great deal of serenity.

'Blasphemy and lies! The owner of these fields is probably locked up in his house with all his people trembling with fear lest your mob decides to attack.'

'And who are you to judge, big man? You and your monasteries and churches get fatter by the day, whilst the poor people starve all around you.'

'We work hard to put food on our table.'

'Peace. What you say may well be true of your monastery. But I can assure you, around here, in the countryside that surrounds Rome, things are different. While common people suffer year after year from famine, we see the palaces of the bishops, the vineyards of the monasteries and the well-fed faces of the clergy. It isn't right. It has to stop.'

'Do you want the church to take a vow of poverty?' Galen asked softly.

Marozia's eyes widened in surprise as she turned to look at Galen. She'd obviously not been expecting him to get involved in the discussion. Her reaction amused Alcuin, who knew both how curious and insightful Galen could be.

'Why not? Jesus never had any worldly possessions, did he?'

'But Jesus was a single man. The church needs funds to spread the word of God.'

'Why? Why can't missionaries go out into the world like Jesus and his disciples? Why do we need vast palaces for the pope and his hundreds of fat bishops?'

'They help organise and resource the missionaries as well as maintain the existing infrastructure of monasteries and churches.'

'Well, they should spend more of that money on the missionaries and less on themselves. And anything that is left over should be used to look after the poor. But perhaps that is a discussion for another night. Tonight I have come to invite you to our prayers.'

'Your prayers?'

'We hold them at the beginning and end of each day to thank our Lord for looking after us on our pilgrimage. After the prayers, I call upon any who need healing to step forward and I lay hands on them.'

'You heal them?' Galen asked.

'I pray for them and act as a channel for God. If He chooses to heal them, He does. Sometimes it needs a change in the supplicant's attitude before God will act, so it pays never to give up hope.'

'I see.'

'Will you join us?'

'I will,' Galen said and cast a hasty, defiant look towards Alcuin.

Alcuin sighed. He knew his friend well enough to know that he wouldn't be easily deterred from attending, even given his fear of crowds.

'We will all be there.'

Chapter 19

Marozia's followers used the wood they gathered, and more that they hacked from the poplars, to build an enormous bonfire in the middle of the road that filled the air with the scent of woodsmoke as sparks spattered and leapt into the night sky. Even at their distance, and with the bodies of so many people between them, Alcuin's face felt hot. Everyone who gathered around to chant prayers, most of which Alcuin didn't recognise, looked ruddy in the light of the blaze.

Sweat was rolling down the faces of the people too, especially those at the front, but this wasn't only due to the fire. He'd never seen a group of people put as much energy into their prayers. There was a great deal of shouting. Some people collapsed to the ground, shaking and groaning as their passion carried them away. One woman fell to her knees and started screeching in a language Alcuin had never heard before, whilst the others clustered about her crying out alleluias.

'This is like no church I know.'

'No,' Galen whispered, watching in amazement. 'But nobody can doubt their devotion.'

'What if it's all an act?'

'They seem sincere. I've also heard tell of monks going into holy raptures like the people here.'

'I've seen it, but there was a lot less excitement from the people around.'

Galen would have replied, but at this moment Marozia held up her hands for silence and said in a loud voice, 'Brothers and sisters, step forward, one and all. Step forward if you need something from your Sister Marozia.'

There was considerable pushing and shoving as people raced each other to reach the front.

The first man to make it fell to his knees before Marozia and said, 'Holy Sister Marozia, ask God to heal my back. Please ask Him to do this for me tonight.'

'Ah, Daneo, I will ask. Your devotion is greatly improved. Perhaps tonight God will finally heed your prayers. If not tonight, then we will try again tomorrow, and the day after tomorrow and the day after that. Until God deems you worthy, we will continue to pray. Now my brother,' Marozia said as she placed both her hands on Daneo's head, 'open your heart and pray to God. Oh Father Almighty, hear the prayers of your servant, Daneo. Heal his back so he may work again. Oh God, we beseech you!'

Alcuin watched the crowd with a growing sense of unease. Every eye was on Marozia and the man. Some even appeared to be holding their breath, while others were mouthing prayers. The man quivered in fear and anticipation and Marozia put on a good show of calling down the Holy Spirit. But in the end, nothing happened.

Marozia spoke of great things to come with such passion that the man straightened out a bit and claimed that he was feeling better for the prayer. A great cheer came from the crowd at that pronouncement. Marozia smiled hugely, showing all her teeth, and claimed that progress was being made. Then she called up the next supplicant. The thin woman and her baby, who had travelled with Alcuin, Galen and Brother Bartolo, hurried forward and the whole thing began again as she knelt before Marozia.

The spectacle left Alcuin feeling queasy. Marozia was feeding off desperation. That realisation made him look down at Galen.

He was dismayed but not surprised that Galen was watching everything with wide, hopeful eyes. His hands were clasped in prayer, willing each person who stepped up to Marozia to be healed.

This evening, she was having no success. Alcuin could tell Galen longed to go up to the front and have Marozia heal him. Much as he disliked the idea, Alcuin feared he'd have to help his friend to the front. He had no faith that the woman could heal Galen, so the sooner he knew it too, the better.

But it made him angry at Marozia for doing this to Galen. He lived in such constant pain that now he was filled with yearning. It wasn't fair and, what was worse, she wasn't going to be the person who'd have to deal with Galen's dashed hopes.

Alcuin would have some strong words for her over that. She wasn't going to get away with — Alcuin's thoughts stopped mid-flow. He'd detected movement out of the corner of his eye and slowly turned to see what had distracted him.

At the edge of the group, hanging back in the shadows, was Bartolo, who usually stuck close to Marozia. His behaviour was suspicious as he looked furtively from the group to the shadows and back again. Then, just as it looked like he was going to give up, a man appeared beside him. They held a low-voiced, intense conversation and then the unknown man vanished back into the night.

Bartolo looked about to check he hadn't been noticed. Then he hurriedly merged back into the crowd. They were in such a frenzy that Alcuin doubted any of them had missed the man.

Galen took a step forward, then stopped as he came to the wall of the backs of the people clustered around Marozia. He couldn't force his way through. The time had come, Alcuin thought, and wondered whether he should pretend he hadn't noticed. But no, that would be too cruel. So he nudged Carbo and indicated with a tilt of his head that they should help Galen.

The big man shook his head imploringly, and Alcuin said, 'With or without us, he's going to do this. The least we can do is help.'

'I don't like it!' Carbo said, but stepped to one side of Galen whilst Alcuin took up position on the other side and they forced their way through the crowd, supporting Galen.

'Ah, my little Brother Galen,' Marozia said and held out her arms in welcome. 'Your need is indeed great. Come, kneel before me and we will ask God to heal you.'

Alcuin helped Galen to kneel, and then he and Carbo took a couple of steps back. The crowd held their breath, as if aware that here was the possibility of a truly great miracle.

Marozia held her hands up to the heavens and said, 'My Lord, Almighty God, heal your humble servant Galen. He has suffered so much already. Take pity on him!'

Then Marozia placed her hands on Galen's head. She gasped, her eyes flew open and with a moan she collapsed to her knees.

'Oh my child, what terrible pain!'

She wrapped her arms around Galen and wept. Alcuin and the audience were stunned. The crowd stood, shifting on their feet, uncertain of what to do. Marozia was supposed to heal the young monk, not be brought low by him. Alcuin tensed, ready to run for Galen and sweep him to safety should the crowd suddenly turn nasty.

Marozia sighed, wiped the tears from her eyes, kissed Galen on either cheek and pushed herself back onto her feet. She smiled at the people, but to Alcuin it looked forced and it failed to hide her shock.

'My people, God has given me a sign tonight, but it wasn't the one I was expecting. It was a reminder that I am His servant, and He will do as He pleases. I beg of you all, go to bed now. I will see you again in the morning.'

The pronouncement left the people unfulfilled. They turned away, muttering their discontent. Alcuin watched them go with the realisation that a mob was a difficult beast to please. In the blink of an eye, universal adulation could pivot to something darker.

Not that Marozia seemed to care. She turned back to Galen, still on his knees where she'd left him, and held her hand out to him.

'Come, we need to talk.'

Alcuin was all too familiar with dealing with Galen's dashed hopes. The last thing they needed was Marozia making things worse.

'He has nothing to say to you.'

'I think he does,' Marozia said, her voice brittle, despite the smile. 'You didn't tell me that Brother Galen is special to God.'

'I don't know what you're talking about.'

Alcuin kept to himself that if a person was supposed to be a saint, he'd expect one to know another. Then again, Galen seemed equally unable to judge anything about Marozia.

'Oh, you don't know? You who have been with him for so long. You who shadow him like a faithful hound keeping harm away from him.'

'If I was keeping harm away from him, I would keep you at a distance too.'

'No, don't,' Galen said and laid his hand on Alcuin's arm. 'Please don't argue. I want to talk to her.'

'Don't let her get to you, Galen!' Alcuin whispered in his ear, trying to convey his alarm as fully as possible.

'It's alright. I won't.'

Alcuin examined Galen's face closely. He looked exhausted. It was probably from their long walk - it was more than he usually did - but there was more.

'What just happened?'

'I don't know. That's why I want to talk to Marozia.'

'Very well, I'll wait.'

Alcuin put his hand on the small of Carbo's back and pushed him along till they were out of hearing of Galen and Marozia.

'We shouldn't be doing this,' Carbo muttered.

'I don't like it either. But we can't help Galen with this saint business. So he will continue to try to find his answers where he may. And if we stood in his way, we would only leave him wondering for the rest of his days about what he could have learned from Marozia.'

'All the same.'

Alcuin nodded, then he noticed Bartolo watching Galen and Marozia with an unreadable expression in his eye that troubled him.

'Brother Carbo. Will you keep watch over Galen, please? There's something I need to check.'

'Don't you worry,' Carbo said with fervour, 'I'll make sure no harm comes to Brother Galen.'

Galen was more disappointed than he thought he'd be. His sensible side had told him over and over again that there was no way Marozia could do anything for him. Just as she'd not really done anything for the people ahead of him. It was amazing how hope could still build a person up to such a height that when nothing came from the encounter he felt crushed. He was shaken too, for he'd not expected Marozia to suffer when she touched him.

'So,' Marozia said as she sat cross-legged opposite Galen and leaned towards him. 'What are you?'

'What do you mean?'

The question surprised him. It implied more than just being a monk. It also made him look around at the people who were being pushed back, so that an ever-widening circle formed around him and Marozia. Only a few looked back. The others were wrapping their meagre clothing around themselves and curling up to sleep, mostly near the bonfire that was still burning away, heating and expanding the resin inside, causing branches to crack apart and shoot out sparks.

'I have had many people before me, Brother Galen. Some I have healed, some not. But I have never felt anything when I do it.'

'Nothing at all?'

This matched Galen's own experience and provided a modicum of comfort. As did the fact that Marozia's prayers were also not always answered by God.

'Nothing,' Marozia said. 'They either go away feeling better or they continue to suffer. But this evening, when I put my hands on your head, I felt such pain... your pain.'

'You felt my pain?'

It sounded miraculous to Galen, but a puzzling miracle. Why would God hurt someone who was trying to heal?

'And there wasn't a thing I could do about it,' Marozia said. 'I am sorry for you.'

Galen nodded and, since his knees had started to ache in the kneeling position, he slid over till he was resting on his hip and straightened his legs out before him.

'There doesn't seem to be a thing I can do about it either, no matter how much I pray to God.'

'Can nobody help you?'

'Some healers have made it better, and some have made it worse. But they were all the efforts of man.'

'I see.' Marozia stared at Galen till he could no longer take it and looked down. 'There is more.'

Galen gave a slight puff of a laugh. This woman really was insightful. Just like his mother.

'I have... I have healed some people. The first two I didn't believe it was me. Like you, I felt nothing. But they claimed to be healed and I couldn't bring them to believe I had nothing to do with it.'

'And the third?'

Galen's gaze flicked briefly to Alcuin, perhaps for reassurance or permission to tell a tale that belonged to both of them. But he was gone and Galen could only see Carbo's deeply disapproving face.

'The third I could not deny. He was dying, I knew that, and yet in the morning he rose without a mark on him.'

'I see. I have never been able to heal anyone at death's door,' Marozia said, casting a thoughtful glance towards where Alcuin had been.

Maybe it was best that he was nowhere to be seen for the moment.

'Can you heal yourself?' Galen asked.

'I have never been so injured that I have wished it. Any slight injuries I receive heal of their own accord, as is the way of nature. Although I prayed for relief when I gave birth to my son, for the pain was extreme. Nothing came of that.'

'I see. Is your son here?'

'He died in the fighting to get rid of the antipope, John. A pointless power struggle amongst nobles that destroyed so many lives and so many livelihoods.'

'Is that what drives you to Rome?'

'It is a part of it.'

Galen nodded as a more uncomfortable thought wriggled its way into his mind.

'Do you really heal anyone at all?'

'I heal their hearts and their souls. For a time, it makes their physical burden easier to bear as well.'

'And they adore you for it.'

'They do.'

'Doesn't that weigh on you? The burden of expectation can be the hardest thing to deal with, especially if you can't heal everyone.'

'Is that what weighs you down?'

'They say only saints perform miracles.'

'And magicians in league with the Devil perform spells which can have the look of miracles.'

Galen shuddered.

'I have no wish to be branded as either.'

'No, but you'd do well to choose one of the two and stick to it.'

'But I am no saint,' Galen wailed, feeling like a thwarted child. 'I can't live a good and blameless life. I am full of pettiness and dissatisfaction.'

Marozia laughed at this outburst and said, 'You can't continue as you always have and leave the decision of what you are to others.'

'They have expectations.'

'That is not the point. Let that be their burden, not yours.'

'I don't want to let them down!'

'My child,' Marozia said, suddenly deathly serious as she leaned forward and took a firm grasp of Galen's hand, 'you cannot move this way and that trying to satisfy the desires of others. Down that path lies only madness. You have to work out what you want and then you have to hold fast to it, despite others' desires. Do you understand?'

Galen nodded, but he could not fully commit and tried to withdraw his hand.

'No,' Marozia said, tightening her grip. 'If I can perform one miracle for you, it is this. You must understand how important it is to be true to yourself. Do not be swayed by others' expectations. Galen, you have to be strong about this one thing above all else.'

'I will try.'

'If you fail, your life will be destroyed. Do you understand?'

'I think so.'

Marozia's gaze remained fixed on Galen's face for so long that he could no longer hold it.

'You have more inner strength than you give yourself credit for, and I have spoken more than enough. You will find your own way.'

Galen doubted it, but there was no point in saying so, especially as Alcuin had reappeared and was making his determined way over.

'Where have you been?' Galen murmured as Alcuin helped him to his feet, Carbo hovering behind.

'Call of nature,' Alcuin said briefly.

He didn't know why, but Galen didn't believe Alcuin and was shocked that his friend would lie so blatantly. But there would be time enough later on to find out what was going on. He gave Marozia a slight bow as she, too, rose to her feet, dusting off her skirts.

'I learned a lot from you. Thank you.'

CHAPTER 20

The return of the intense smell of woodsmoke signalled to Galen that it was morning and the rest of the party was up. So he no longer needed to try to get the sleep that had remained elusive all night. He lay on his side, tightly wrapped in his cloak since the morning was chilly, watching the crowd. They had gathered before another enormous bonfire, similar to the one of last night, for their morning prayers. The smoke from the fire merged with the mist that filled the valley.

Maybe it was the mist that damped the sound, but the cultists appeared more subdued than the night before. Maybe it was just because sleep still clung to the people's minds or because of the anticlimactic ending to the previous night; either way they seemed deflated.

Galen decided not to ascribe too much importance to himself. Others wouldn't feel as disturbed as he did. And all night he'd had far too many thoughts churning around and around in his head to even be able to sleep.

By dawn, though, he'd come to a better understanding of Marozia and her actions. Maybe she did have a gift and maybe she could heal people, but that wasn't the important thing. What was important to her and what she valued was how she related to her gift and how she used it.

She was a charismatic woman. People flocked to her and so she used her gift to help those in need in a very public way. Because she had their attention, she could also bend their wills to do what she wished. And because she was a persuasive speaker, perhaps she could get people to believe it was their will too.

Galen realised that for others, it was just a safe haven. A place where someone ordered their lives, told them what to do, and helped them through the day. People who'd lost a great deal found it hard to think for themselves, Galen knew that only too well. It was a comfort to find someone who would do their thinking for them.

To his surprise, Galen didn't want that from Marozia. He didn't want it from anyone. Not anymore. It was time to think for himself. It was time he grew up.

His belly clenched in fright at the very idea, but he was on that path now and there would be no deviation. Galen looked around some more and spotted Alcuin preparing breakfast from what remained in their bag. Well, maybe some things could still be ordered by other people, Galen thought as he smiled up at Alcuin.

'You're in a good mood then, are you?' Alcuin said as he handed over the bread and cheese and settled beside Galen.

'I had an interesting talk with Marozia.'

'It left you so thoughtful you barely had two words for me and Carbo last night.'

'I'm sorry,' Galen said and flushed with the sense that he'd let his friend down.

Alcuin laughed and gave his shoulder a friendly pat.

'Don't worry, it's merely jealousy on my part that Marozia could command so much of your attention.'

'You warned me against her.'

'She's very charismatic.'

'And I am easily taken in?'

'You always see the best in people.'

'Except Carbo.'

'His build worked against him, but you've taken to him too, haven't you?'

Galen nodded and looked around for the big man. Much to his surprise, he saw the monk deep in discussion with the oldest of the priests Marozia had in her entourage.

'He's actually engaging with them?'

'Well...' Alcuin said and scratched his head in the way he had when he was still considering what to say.

'What's going on?' Galen asked, remembering that Alcuin had been evasive the night before too.

'I'm not exactly sure.'

Alcuin drew closer to Galen, keeping his back to Marozia's followers. He had all the appearance of a man making sure they weren't overheard, even though it was highly doubtful any of the cultists could understand Englisc.

'Last night, I noticed Bartolo slipping out of the crowd. It could have been nothing, a call of nature—'

'As you claimed for yourself last night,' Galen murmured, giving Alcuin a pointed look.

'Sorry, I didn't want to say something in front of Carbo or Marozia. Not till I'd discussed it with you anyhow.'

'So what happened?'

Galen's overactive imagination came up with a hundred and one possibilities, none of them good.

'I don't know for sure, but Bartolo secretly met with somebody. A warrior-like man who remained hidden amongst the trees while they talked. It looked like it got quite heated. Then after a while, the other man left on horseback and rode off towards Rome.'

'That is strange.'

'That isn't all,' Alcuin said, casting a look over his shoulder.

Galen could have reassured him that nobody was looking their way.

'Bartolo rejoined Brother Gentile. Despite having claimed a vow of silence, the two of them had a long, whispered conversation, all with the appearance of trying to keep it hidden.'

'That is strange indeed.'

Galen was about to start formulating theories when Carbo returned, looking graver than usual. Considering how displeased he was to be following along in the cult's wake, this was doubly concerning.

'Well?' Alcuin asked, then turned to Galen with an explanation. 'I asked Brother Carbo to find out as much as he could about Marozia.'

'It's nothing good,' Carbo said in a whisper. 'It paid to talk to an old priest though. He had all sorts of information he remembered from his youth.'

'About what?' Galen asked, feeling his shoulders tensing, for they looked like a trio of conspirators huddled together, whispering to each other.

'Have either of you ever heard of the Rule of the Harlots?' Carbo asked, flushing to mention something so potentially inflammatory.

Galen had a vague feeling he'd heard the phrase before, but he couldn't quite remember it. Alcuin just shook his head, but then Galen's memory found what he'd been looking for.

'Oh, I know! I once copied something out on the history of the popes back at Yarmwick. There were certain allusions made to undue influence by a mother and a daughter over the papacy. But it was all very vague. Is that what you are referring to?'

'I am not a very well educated man,' Carbo said. 'All I know of the popes is that none seems to last very long and there are always battles over their successors. What I learned today almost puts me in sympathy with Marozia's wish to tear the system down.'

'Actually, she just wants the pope to share some of the wealth,' Galen said.

'How would you do that without tearing everything down?'

'We are straying from the point,' Alcuin said.

'True.' Carbo stuffed the remains of his breakfast into his mouth and chewed for a bit. 'That old priest told me that two women, one Theodora, and her daughter Marozia...'

'Marozia?' Galen said.

'This cult leader,' Carbo said, pointing over his shoulder at the cultists, 'is the great-granddaughter of the same family, the... the—'

'Theophylacti!' Galen was astonished that some dry piece of history he'd transcribed in the shadowy scriptorium of Yarmwick was suddenly leaping to vivid life. 'An extremely powerful family based in Rome. Or so my history said. Several popes came from within the family.'

'The priest said that Marozia the elder became one of the pope's concubines when she was fifteen. She had numerous affairs with several popes, had some of them assassinated and even got her son onto the papal throne. The influence of those two harlots only ended upon the death of Pope John XII.'

'Ah, even I've heard of him,' Alcuin said. 'He's infamous for his corruption. This is alarming news indeed.'

Carbo nodded hearty agreement.

'Bad enough that they're a cult. But what if this Marozia is trying to reclaim the power her family amassed? If anything, papal politics is a hundred times deadlier than some cult. We really should distance ourselves from them.'

'I have learned all I can from Marozia,' Galen said. 'There is no need to remain with them. They walk faster than I can manage anyway so, we can just let them pull ahead. Although it will take some while for a substantial gap to form.'

'True, but let's also give them some time to pack up and go before we set off,' Alcuin said. 'We aren't in such a rush to get to Rome that we need to leave immediately.'

Galen nodded agreement and took a thoughtful bite of his bread, looking around.

'But you know... isn't it too quiet this morning?'

'You call that quiet?' Carbo said, tilting his chin in the direction of the cult followers who had warmed up and reached the point in their prayers where two women were writhing on the ground, speaking in tongues.

'No, not them.' Galen pointed down the road where the mist was starting to thin and had taken on a golden hue. 'There's nobody else around, not a soul. Surely we should already have merchants and all the other travellers, as we did yesterday. But nobody has appeared from either direction.'

'Lord have mercy!' Carbo jumped up and scanned the road towards Rome over the heads of the cultists. 'You're right: it's empty.'

'What does that mean?' Alcuin asked, also getting up.

'Nothing good!'

Carbo grabbed Galen's arm and hauled him to his feet.

'What's going on?' Galen said at the same time as Alcuin.

'Something's definitely wrong,' Carbo said and dragged Galen down the road. 'We need to get as far as we can from Marozia and her people.'

'Be careful, for God's sake,' Alcuin shouted, 'or you'll do Galen an injury.'

'Things could be a lot worse if we don't get away from that bunch,' Carbo said as he practically hoisted Galen's feet off the ground.

'But what is it?' Galen gasped as the air was knocked out of him with every step.

'It could be nothing, but my soldier's instincts are screaming ambush. If I was going to take out the cultists, especially if I didn't want anyone to know about it, I'd block the road off first.'

His words were so shocking that dizziness overwhelmed Galen.

'There, listen,' Carbo said, breaking into a run. 'Horses at full gallop. This is bad.'

As he spoke, a group of heavily armed and armoured riders burst through the mist.

'They aren't slowing, although they must see Marozia's people,' Alcuin shouted.

'Aye!'

Carbo came to an abrupt halt and pushed Galen behind his vast bulk as he took up a sturdy stance, his staff clutched in both hands.

Alcuin had only enough time to do the same, keeping Galen between the two of them. A cry of panic went up as the soldiers lowered their lances. The cry turned into a wail of terror and pain as the lances tore into the cultists.

Galen braced himself, unable to take his eyes off the massacre and feeling like a coward because he was relieved to have Carbo and Alcuin protecting him. But what could they do against a well armed cavalry? As little as Marozia's people, who had formed a protective barrier around their leader.

The men in that group were lightly armed with staves. One had a sickle that he was waving wildly about himself, another had a short heavy blade of the sort used to prune the branches off trees. None had any weapon that could go against the lances and swords of the soldiers. Behind them were the monks and priests who had led the morning prayers. Bartolo was right beside Marozia, white-faced, with only the short dagger he used for eating in his hand.

'No!' Galen shouted as the leader of the soldiers twisted about on his horse.

He'd spotted Marozia. Now he shouted orders to a band of his men, ramming his heels into his mount as the cavalry crashed into the huddle of Marozia's protectors. Some were run through with spears, others hacked at, more still were knocked down and trampled under the horses' hooves.

Marozia turned to run, but Bartolo grabbed her plait, pulled her towards him and plunged his dagger into her back. Then he dropped the dagger and held his bloody hands in the air in surrender.

The commander kicked Bartolo, sending him flying flat on his face, ran him over, then wheeled his horse around and ran over Marozia's prone body before thrusting his lance through her, whilst his men dealt with the rest.

Galen was so horrified that he didn't realise a knight was riding full tilt at their little group until Carbo gave a roar and grounded himself. As the man hurtled past, Carbo batted the lance away and, with a mighty swing of his staff, knocked the soldier off his mount. The horse carried on; the man rolled over and over, his armour clattering on the stone.

'Come,' Carbo shouted, 'we can't hang about here.'

He threw Galen over his shoulder and ran for the scrubby growth by the side of the river. Carbo leapt through the undergrowth, pushing through rank, long grass. Alcuin bounded along behind, squelching and sliding through the mud. They waded on for a way before Carbo dropped to the ground.

'Are you alright, Brother Galen?'

Galen looked at him in wide-eyed horror as he fought to get his breath back, then he gave a quick nod.

'How about you, Brother Alcuin?'

'I'm fine,' Alcuin said between gasps of air. 'What the devil is happening?'

'Looks like somebody powerful didn't want Marozia to get to Rome,' Carbo whispered over the screams of people.

'Why in heaven's name not?'

'How would I know? Rome is a crazy city. I can't wait to get back to my monastery.'

Galen was shaking so much he feared he'd give them away by setting the reeds about him to trembling. Alcuin looked little better. But when he realised he was being watched, he forced a grimace to convey that he was alright, or as alright as he could be under the circumstances.

'We should have guessed it would be that way. It will be similar to Lundenburh, I suppose.'

'It will be like nothing you know,' Carbo said. 'In Rome, they fight over who will be the next emperor and who will have dominion over our souls. You have no idea—' Carbo stopped abruptly and pushed Galen's head down into the mud as he ducked his own head.

They held their breath as a horse rode slowly past their hiding place, the crack of its hooves loud on the paving stones. There wasn't much left of the shouting. It seemed Marozia's band was dispersed or dead.

Carbo let go of Galen's head and whispered, 'It sounds like they're leaving.'

'How can you tell?' Galen asked, because he could still hear wailing.

'No more clash of arms. Just the cry of the injured. I'm guessing only from the injured soldiers. The cultists will all be dead.'

Galen nodded, and they lay in silence, their heads down. Galen's heart was hammering so hard in his chest he was certain it could be heard by the others, although they were both also breathing so heavily, while trying not to be heard, that they probably wouldn't notice.

After a while, Galen started to notice the other sounds around him: the buzz of insects, the lapping of the river water and even the wind blowing through the remaining clattering yellow and brown poplar leaves.

'They've left,' Carbo said, but stayed lying in the mud.

'How did they know?' Galen asked.

'How did they know what?'

'That Marozia was coming.'

'They were told, and I think I know by whom,' Alcuin said. 'It was that damned Bartolo.'

'The slimy pigswill was looking out for himself,' Carbo muttered.

'He killed Marozia,' Galen said, and it pained him to say that the woman was dead.

'He did?' Alcuin said. 'Good Lord, how do you know that?'

'I saw it. You and Carbo were protecting us, but I saw Bartolo grab Marozia and stab her.'

'That worthless dog,' Carbo growled.

'I thought you didn't like Marozia.'

'I didn't. But I didn't wish to see her killed either. Not like this. If she did something wrong, they should have taken her before a judge.'

Galen gave a slight nod and said, 'Do you think it's safe to get out of this mud now?'

Carbo cocked his head and listened, then holding his hand out to indicate the others should wait, he inched through the reeds and peered out into the road. Galen held his breath. They'd be dead if they were caught.

'Looks like they're gone.'

'Good,' Alcuin said as he heaved himself to his feet and helped Galen get up out of the sucking mud.

Galen staggered out onto the path, and his eyes swept the road. It was littered with bodies. People that only moments before had been singing and praying and making plans for the days ahead. It made Galen so sick his knees buckled under him.

'Galen!' Alcuin cried and bent down to check his face. 'Are you alright?'

Galen nodded, but tears made rivulets down his cheeks. 'They didn't deserve this.'

'They didn't,' Carbo said as he came up beside Galen and took his other side, lifting him to his feet.

Much as he feared seeing her body, Galen looked to where he'd last seen Marozia. Maybe it was because of the chaos of battle, or maybe his memory was disturbed by events, but she wasn't where he'd expected. He staggered towards the bodies of her protectors, making the sign of the cross and whispering the last rites, encompassing everyone.

Alcuin leaned over the body of one monk in a bleached habit and dusted the ash from his face to reveal the silent Brother Gentile.

'Bartolo's not here.'

'Neither is Marozia,' Galen said, and a faint hope flickered that maybe she'd survived.

Then a flurry of ash swirled past, carrying the scent of woodsmoke from the remains of the morning's bonfire. Galen turned towards it and his worst fears were confirmed.

There was a body lying face down in the ashes, her bloodstained tan dress smouldering.

'Marozia!'

Galen hurried to the woman and tried to roll her body over, but it was heavy. The fire was still hot and he burned the back of his hand on a glowing coal.

'I'll do it.'

Carbo pulled Galen back, then lifted Marozia's body out of the ash and laid her face up on the road. Her blue eyes were wide open and caked with ash. A sob burst from Galen as, with trembling hands, he closed her eyes and made the sign of the cross over her.

Alcuin put a reassuring hand on Galen's shoulder as he looked down at the woman.

'She didn't stand a chance.'

'How could they? She may not have been a saint, and her methods may have been manipulative, but she meant well. She didn't deserve this!'

Carbo nodded absentminded agreement, but his attention was on the road. Galen assumed he was on the lookout for knights in case they came back. Then he looked back down at Galen, kneeling in ash that was stained red with Marozia's blood. His eyes widened in horror, as if he were seeing Galen for the first time.

'Holy tears of God, the dream!' he bellowed. 'We have to get away now!' He swooped down on Galen, lifted him in both arms and ran as fast as his legs could carry him across the road and back into cover.

Alcuin hammered after him, shouting, 'Carbo, come back. What the devil's got into you?'

'Hide!'

Carbo plunged through the undergrowth and this time right into the river.

'No, what are you doing?' Galen asked, battering against the big man's chest. 'I can't swim.'

'You'll be alright,' Carbo whispered. 'But believe me, we're in danger. Keep still.'

Galen subsided immediately as Alcuin splashed into the water and joined them. They were now just three heads, barely breaking the surface of the water amongst the reeds, and Carbo was pushing along the river. He looked like every sense was on high alert as he dragged Galen with him. His behaviour was so peculiar that Galen could only be glad that Alcuin was still with them and could provide a modicum of protection.

Then they heard hundreds of men on the march.

'Surely they can't all have been sent after Marozia,' Alcuin hissed.

'Probably not,' Carbo whispered. 'There must be more afoot. Either way, if they find us, we're dead.'

'Which way are they heading?'

'Sounds like they are going away from Rome. But I don't know what that means. I am just a simple monk from an insignificant monastery.'

'Not so simple,' Galen said through chattering teeth.

'Are you cold?'

'The water is a little cold, but it's more fear and shock.'

'Can you stand staying in the water?'

Galen nodded and then they all subsided into silence as they heard voices near them on the road.

Carbo didn't move for hours, and Galen and Alcuin, after exchanging a couple of glances, followed his lead. After all, he had far more experience of war than they did.

As the sun was heading for midday and the sound of soldiers had long since tailed away, Carbo whispered, 'You two stay here. I'm going to take a look around. Don't move till I get back. If I'm not back by nightfall, assume the worst and head for Rome without me.'

He didn't stop to see what effect his words had, just pulled himself out of the water and made his cautious way through the reeds.

'I hope he doesn't take long,' Galen said.

The barges had returned to the river and Galen wondered whether the boaters could see them, as the reeds behind them were considerably thinner than those towards the land. Fortunately, none of the men on the boats made any sign of spotting them.

It was afternoon before Carbo reappeared and helped Alcuin haul Galen onto dry land.

'You'd best sit here in the sun for a while to dry off and get warm. It looks like the water has chilled you all the way through.'

'As long as it hasn't damaged my books, I don't mind.'

Galen's lips were so cold he could hardly shape them to speak.

'Do you know what's going on, Carbo?' Alcuin asked.

'An army went through for certain, heading away from Rome. I don't know what that means for our arrival there, but they cleared the road. There are no signs of bodies.'

Alcuin and Galen nodded, too cold and tired to worry about something in the future.

Then Galen decided to ask the question that had preoccupied him during his long, cold wait.

'You shouted about the dream before you hauled us away.'

'Oh that,' Carbo said and flushed.

Alcuin's eyebrows rose in surprise.

'What? Do you think this was the dream Fra' Arnal had? That Marozia would be killed?'

'You know about it?' Carbo said in surprise.

'Ah yes, sorry, I overheard Fra' Arnal telling you about it.'

'So you have always known why I was with you?'

'I have. I didn't tell Galen until much later.'

'And I ignored it,' Galen said with an apologetic smile. 'I didn't want to attach too much importance to a dream.'

'Fra' Arnal doesn't make things up.' Carbo looked discomforted and offended that his abbot wasn't believed. 'He was certain God spoke to him. So sure, he sent me to protect you.'

'He thought God spoke to him?'

'He isn't a man who is prone to visions. Although the dream wasn't precisely what happened.'

'It's an allegory of sorts,' Galen said as he frowned and lapsed into deep thought.

'An allegory?'

Alcuin waited for Galen to answer but when he didn't, he said, 'A dream to show that Galen was in trouble and would need help. We will always be grateful that your abbot sent you. You made our journey much easier and if you hadn't hauled us into hiding this morning, we might have died.'

'Fra' Arnal's dream also said I'd been travelling to Rome all my life,' Galen said, his frown deepening. 'But I never wanted to go to Rome.'

'But maybe God wants you there,' Carbo said.

'Maybe. Either way, there is no sense in remaining here,' Galen said as he pushed himself to his feet. 'We'd better get moving.'

Despite Carbo's reassurance that the road was now clear, a tremor washed over Galen as he emerged from the undergrowth.

What met his gaze, though, was surreal. All the traffic, the carts, loaded mules and pedestrians were back, walking along the road as if nothing had happened. There were no bodies, no ash, not even a single bloodstain.

'What is all this?' Alcuin murmured as he looked up and down the road.

'It's as if Marozia and her followers never existed,' Galen said.

'For the sake of our survival, it would be best never to mention her again either,' Alcuin said and helped Galen up the slight incline so that he was now fully on the road. 'And we should do nothing to draw attention, especially here. Who knows whether they have left spies to make sure no-one escaped?'

'Good point,' Carbo said. 'Let's make haste to Rome.'

Chapter 21

Galen was overwhelmed by what had happened, especially on a day that had started so calmly. This wasn't his first battle, but it felt the most devastating. Maybe because it had come from nowhere. Maybe because it had been aimed at helpless people. Maybe because of the ruthless expunging of lives. These people weren't just killed, they were disappeared. Why would anyone want to make it seem like they had never even existed?

Galen could think of only one reason: because it was a crime. Only a murderer hid the body of his victim. How much worse to hide over a hundred bodies.

Galen glanced up at Alcuin and then Carbo. Their expressions were equally grim. Alcuin, especially, looked very pale.

'Are you alright?'

Alcuin looked surprised, then shook it away and gave a wan smile.

'It was a terrible morning. More importantly, though, how are you?'

It was typical Alcuin, always worrying about his friend over himself. Galen was in pain. Being thrown about, running, and spending a few hours in cold water, had played havoc with his guts. It meant his walking had slowed because every step jarred.

'I'll be fine in a little while.' Galen looked about them at the other users of the road and said, 'They look like nothing happened.'

'As far as they know, nothing did. Although they must be curious about why this important road to Rome was blocked. It might also be my imagination, but I feel we are being given more space than before.'

'Why would that be?'

'Probably because we're monks,' Carbo said. 'Armies might try to hide what is happening from the people, but word gets out.'

'Word about what?'

'Cults... monks...' Carbo shrugged.

Galen nodded.

'The road was blocked and rumours about a cult must have been abroad, so they're playing it safe.'

'It's what I would do.'

'Yes, I suppose so. There is much to trouble me about this morning, and it seems we are not the only ones after all.'

'Best never to mention it again,' Carbo said.

Galen had become used to the big monk's lack of curiosity. But it wasn't something he could suppress so easily in himself.

'From my experience, if you want to stop something like a cult from spreading, you need to make an example of them. Like they did to Geoffroi the Heretic. He and his people were tried, executed, and their bodies put on display. The only reason you hide something, and go to such lengths as we saw, is because what you are doing is against the law.'

'Or they don't have enough evidence.'

Alcuin could be relied upon to engage in supposition and enquiry. It was how the two of them had whiled away many an hour.

'If they're powerful enough to block a major trade route they would have no difficulty in fabricating evidence.'

Galen had seen it often enough as the son of a noble and had seen similar deception even within the church.

'True,' Alcuin said, tilting his head to consider. 'The more you think about it, the odder it becomes.'

'And then there's Bartolo,' Galen said, but reluctantly, as it brought back the vivid memory of the morning. 'Why did he stab Marozia?'

Carbo came to an abrupt halt.

'You are not taking my warning seriously. Don't mention that woman's name. Not out here in the open, not even when you believe yourself to be alone. Same goes for that man.'

'But he stabbed her,' Galen said, checking the passersby, who looked oblivious to their conversation. 'Why would he do that?'

'Probably to save his own skin,' Carbo said in a tone that indicated they should stop. 'He thought if he killed her, they might let him go.'

'But then he was ridden over.'

Galen lowered his voice even though he worried that made them all look too conspiratorial, especially as Alcuin's eyes widened in amazement.

'But his body wasn't amongst the dead,' Alcuin said. 'Maybe he'd been working against Ma— you know who, all along.'

'Why do you say that?'

'I don't know. He just felt a bit off to me. But maybe that was because he was unlikeable.'

Galen nodded. Bartolo had not tried to make friends or win favours. He'd been brusque and kept to himself. Even, thinking back to the day they'd spent with the cult, distancing the cult members from their leader by pushing them away from her.

Galen had assumed it was so that Marozia could have some peace from the constant barrage of requests from her followers. Now he wondered whether Bartolo was trying to separate them from her.

It had been the same with the followers he'd gathered along their journey. He'd returned with only a handful of people. But again, Galen hadn't seen him trying to recruit anyone before they'd reached Marozia.

He'd ignored the people who followed him, as if he didn't care about them. Maybe that wasn't the truth. Maybe he'd not wanted them to join the cult in the first place.

But when questioned about Marozia, he'd defended her and spoken as if her actions were just. So why grab her, keeping her within reach of the soldiers, and stab her? It made no sense.

Maybe Carbo was right: he'd just been trying to save himself. Galen couldn't convince himself that was the case. Then again, with all the followers dead, he had no hope of ever discovering the truth.

Galen would have liked to continue his discussion with Alcuin, but Carbo looked so furious that he subsided into silence. His curiosity had got him into trouble before and it was wise to exercise restraint. After all, the big man had been a soldier and knew more about how they might operate. If he was this worried, it was best to keep quiet.

The problem with not chatting was that Galen focused on the pain. At first, he tried to distract himself with the view. As they were getting closer to Rome, the land was becoming more hilly and the country estates more imposing. The land was also more heavily cultivated, and grape vines proliferated.

But the scenery wasn't a sufficient distraction, so Galen switched to watching the passersby. Almost all of them were faster than Galen and his companions. If it weren't for him, Alcuin and Carbo would surely already have reached Rome.

They might never have joined Marozia's band either. Galen shook away that guilty thought and went back to people-watching. Now that the sun had come out, many of them had taken off their cloaks and slung them over a shoulder, or draped them across their carts. It was amazing how much warmer these southern countries were, and Galen was feeling a little over-warm himself, especially with the woollen cloak from his father.

He was just about to request a halt so he could remove his cloak when a pebble hit his cheek. Galen stopped and looked around. Sometimes a horse might kick up a chip of stone as it ran past, but other than that, there was no explanation. And there was no galloping horse, something Galen had become hyper-aware of. Then a second pebble struck his shoulder, and a third skittered across the ground at his feet.

'What is that?'

'What is what?' Carbo asked.

'Someone is throwing stones at me,' Galen said as he examined a dense clump of trees dominated by a black spindle-shaped cypress.

'Why would someone throw stones at you?' Alcuin said, peering into the dim interior.

Just then, another pebble flew out of the bushes and hit Galen's cloak.

'See!'

'Probably some unruly child,' Carbo said, tutting in irritation. 'Just ignore him.'

It sounded plausible, but another larger stone hit Galen's robe.

'Don't children run away once they're discovered?'

'They usually do,' Alcuin said and walked into the deep shade of the spinney.

Galen was glad he'd acted so decisively, otherwise Carbo would have dragged them away without ever resolving the mystery. As it was, Carbo didn't budge and held on to Galen so that he couldn't follow Alcuin. Not that Galen would take more steps than absolutely necessary.

'You'd better take a look,' Alcuin said from the shadows.

His expression was unexpectedly grave, and he was speaking softly.

'Mother of God, what now?' Carbo muttered, but helped Galen off the smooth path and down the slight dip into the copse. 'Holy Mary, Mother of God!' he added as he and Galen spotted the figure on the ground.

He was propped up against a pine tree, his legs sprawled out before him. Blood was liberally splattered across his faded habit and his face was as white as vellum and beaded with sweat.

'Bartolo?!' Galen gasped and froze, incapable of getting any closer to the man.

Bartolo gave them all a weak smile.

'I see you survived.'

'And you,' Carbo said, also keeping his distance.

'But in less good shape.' Bartolo raised his right arm and waved it vaguely at the rest of his body. 'My left arm is shattered, as are several ribs.'

'But you got away,' Alcuin said. 'How did you manage that?'

His suspicion was understandable, Galen thought, for he was wondering the same.

'I played dead,' Bartolo said, his voice soft and shaky. 'And when the knights took their leave, I crawled away into the undergrowth. Then I ran. I didn't expect that another group would be sent along to clean everything up. Fortunately, I'd put some distance between myself and them by that time and managed to get this far before my injuries overcame me.'

'So, what do you want from us?' Carbo said in a hard, uncompromising tone.

'Would it be too much to ask for help from a group of fellow monks?'

'You are no monk. You are a traitor who abandoned his order to join a cult. You earned this punishment.'

'I dare say you're right,' Bartolo said with a wry smile, looking straight at Galen, 'but could a saint leave a man to die by the side of the road?'

'How do you know?' Galen asked.

'Marozia told me. She was quite amused. She said she'd never expected to meet an actual saint.'

'How dare you even bring up her name after what you did?'

An unaccustomed rage was burning through Galen, fuelled by Bartolo's lack of remorse.

'What did I do?' Bartolo said, wheezing with the effort of speech.

'You stabbed her,' Galen said, clenching his fists.

'Ah... so you saw that.'

'Did you also betray her?' Alcuin asked.

'What do you think?'

'You met with a horseman last night and then—'

Bartolo held up his hand.

'It seems you were more observant than I'd assumed. More fool me. But then again... I seem to have been fooled by both sides.'

'So you don't deny it?'

Bartolo waved his uninjured arm, as if to say, *why bother?*

'Will you help me?'

'Why should we?' Carbo asked.

'Because you are men of God. Him especially,' Bartolo said, pointing at Galen. 'Could you even leave me here to die?'

That was a good question. Galen couldn't leave the man. He was clearly in a lot of pain and no longer had the strength to get back onto his feet unaided.

'Marozia said you brought somebody back from the brink of death,' Bartolo said.

'God did that,' Galen said, and for the first time in his life, he had no wish to heal someone in need.

'Do you think He will do the same for me?'

'I don't know.'

'You don't deserve it,' Alcuin said.

'You don't know what I deserve,' Bartolo snapped back.

'You're a murderer and a traitor,' Galen said, and it shocked him, for he'd never been so harsh to anyone before.

'You don't know that.'

'After what I saw?'

'That is only half the story.'

'You mean your reason for what you did and who you did it with?'

'Who I did it for. The one who betrayed me.'

'We don't need to know that,' Carbo said. 'Brother Galen, please, this is too dangerous. The less you know in situations like this, the better.'

'I know.'

Galen looked from Bartolo to Carbo, trying to decide what to do. Carbo was right, this wasn't their business. Yet at the same time, he burned to know. For the first time, he understood the blood feuds his people engaged in. He had known Marozia for such a short time, yet she'd left an indelible mark upon him. Maybe that was a sign of her power. He couldn't let her death have been for nothing. He couldn't allow her to be erased from history.

'What can we do though, Brother Carbo? We can't leave him here, for he will surely die.'

'We can report him to the authorities when we arrive in Rome. We're nearly there as it is. He wouldn't have long to wait until they send somebody to find him.'

'That would sign my death warrant too,' Bartolo said.

'If you were tried, you'd be found guilty of murder,' Carbo said. 'Death is all that awaits you anyway.'

'Then you should just leave me here to die in peace,' Bartolo said, and closed his eyes.

Galen looked across at Alcuin, standing closest to the man.

'I don't know,' Alcuin said. 'If he's tried as a murderer, he'll hang for sure.'

'Not if there are no bodies,' Galen said.

'Will you at least get me to the gates of Rome?' Bartolo said as he opened his eyes and looked straight at Galen. 'The knowledge I have will be useful to you since you wish to speak to the pope.'

It was strange to Galen that everyone had turned to him to make a final decision. It wasn't like Alcuin to defer to him, yet even he was waiting.

'If we cover his robe to hide the blood, would you be able to support him up to the gates of Rome, Brother Carbo?'

'Brother Galen, no,' Carbo said, sounding like a child whose hand was being forced. 'I was sent to keep you safe. If we are caught helping this man, they will brand us as conspirators and put us to death. We can't do it.'

'You will gain more by helping me than by abandoning me,' Bartolo said. 'And I know how to keep my mouth shut.'

'Not if you're tortured, you can't.'

'Even if I'm tortured,' Bartolo said, and it sounded to Galen like it might not be the first time.

'If it's about the pope...' Alcuin started, but his uncertainty made his words fade.

'I know it's a risk,' Galen said, 'but I feel we should help, and not because of anything Bartolo is saying, but because he is in need and we are the only ones who can help him.'

'You could help me most by healing me,' Bartolo said.

'No.' Even Galen was surprised by his strength of feeling on the matter. 'I won't touch you.'

'That is showing less than Christian mercy and forgiveness. Shame on you, saint,' Bartolo said in his more usual sardonic tone.

'I am aware, but for you my support will only go so far.'

Chapter 22

Alcuin was happy to take back his role of supporting Galen. It was funny that he resented Carbo for having taken over that function, even when he knew it was sensible to have Carbo help Galen. But now the big monk was half carrying, half walking Bartolo, whom they'd wrapped in Carbo's substantial cape.

They waited in the shadows until the road was clear before stepping out into the open. Then, once they were back in the full glare of the sun, they double-checked that nothing of Bartolo's bloodstained robes was visible.

'This is dangerous,' Alcuin murmured in Englisc so only Galen would hear or understand.

'Carbo was right from the start,' Galen said, looking tense, probably both from pain and fear. 'The moment we joined Marozia's group, we were at risk. But now, whether or not we help is irrelevant. If some higher power was determined to erase her from the face of the earth, then any remaining witness is at risk. Helping Bartolo at this point would make little difference, as we were already witnesses to the massacre.'

'It's unfortunate that he spotted us on the road, otherwise he may have assumed he was the sole remaining survivor.'

Galen shuddered at the thought.

'Then perhaps... perhaps God wanted it this way.'

'It's unusual for you to say such a thing,' Alcuin said, reflecting that Galen had changed a lot.

It had started with the Moors. When they'd been reunited, Galen was a little more independent than he'd been before. After Alcuin's near death, Galen had also seemed different, and even more so after talking to Marozia. She'd apparently given him a lot to think about.

Alcuin felt a tinge of jealousy that it was outsiders and not him who'd had more of an influence on his friend. Maybe he'd been too lazy, or too willing to stick with the status quo, for it gave him power over Galen. He knew he was a bit autocratic, but he'd always done what he thought was best for Galen. Maybe he'd been wrong.

The sun was beginning to set when Carbo said, 'There it is, see?'

Alcuin realised that for the last couple of miles he'd been walking, head down, tired from taking Galen's extra weight. Galen also looked pale, his lips pressed so tightly together they were white.

Alcuin and Galen came to a stop and took a first look at a city Alcuin had never thought he'd see. With the sun behind him, the city looked impressive on the famous seven hills. A massive stone wall encircled a space at least three times the size of Lundenburh. Inside were thick-walled buildings, some built from a dark brick, others from marble that gleamed golden in the setting sun, almost all of them with towers.

'Why so many towers?'

'Some are the defensive towers of the nobility's palaces. The rest are churches,' Carbo said in a disinterested voice. 'They say Rome has more churches than there are days in the year.'

While the information about the churches was interesting, it was the peculiar habits of the nobility that spurred Alcuin's curiosity

'They have castles inside the city?'

'I told you, it's a place like no other. The nobility are constantly at war with each other.'

'Inside the city?'

'Inside and out,' Carbo said, tilting his head at Bartolo, who didn't react to their words.

'Do you think that's what precipitated...' Galen started and then sank into silence because of Carbo's warning look.

He didn't have to finish what he was saying, and Alcuin was relieved that he didn't. Galen was wondering whether a feud between the nobility had resulted in Marozia's death.

'You'll get your answers soon enough,' Carbo said, and hoisted Bartolo higher up in his grip.

The man groaned from the pain of being manhandled. Alcuin looked back down at Galen. He was such a kind and forgiving person who couldn't bear to see anyone suffer that usually he'd have done all he could to help an injured man. But, although he looked discomforted, he still refused to touch Bartolo.

'What would you think if God actually healed him?'

Galen gave him a startled look.

'Do you think I'm being petty?'

'I understand your motives. But if you healed him, it would make it easier for all of us.'

'No,' Galen said in an absolute tone that Alcuin had never heard from him before.

'But what if it was God's will?'

'I cannot believe that. If God healed him... I don't know what I would think then. Besides, God gave us the freedom to make our own choices. I am exercising that right.'

The discussion was veering into dangerous theological territory, so Alcuin subsided into silence and focused on getting the two of them up to the towering gates of Rome. The surrounding travellers had picked up speed, determined not to be trapped outside the city walls come nightfall.

'They're afraid of bandits,' Carbo said, and he also picked up speed. 'This is a wild and dangerous place after dark.'

'Let's hurry then,' Galen said by way of reassuring Alcuin that he could walk faster.

'Stop me if I go too fast,' Alcuin said as he hurried after Carbo.

Galen was gasping by the time they arrived at the Porta Portuensis, so Alcuin had less attention to give to the largest city walls he'd ever seen. They were more than double the height and width of Hatim's fortress, and the entrance was a carved marble with four columns and two alcoves with gigantic stone vases, all of which must have been created by the ancient Romans.

'At least with this crowd rushing for entry, we are less likely to be noticed,' Carbo muttered in Latin.

As it was, one of the guards crooked his finger at the group of monks, calling them out of the crowd.

He said something that neither Alcuin nor Galen understood, and even Carbo seemed to struggle with. Then Bartolo said something in a thin, exhausted voice and the man hastily stepped back from them and waved them in.

'What did you say?' Carbo asked, his voice heavy with suspicion.

'Nothing more than we are travelling monks come to seek healing at a monastery.'

'The way that guard reacted, he looked like he suspected we might be carrying the plague.'

'I told him it was malaria, so he couldn't deny us entry, but that and plague can look similar, hence his caution.'

'Cunning as always,' Carbo muttered and headed for the narrowest of the streets that faced them.

There were three roads fanning out into Rome. They each ran straight as a rule and were paved in the same wide, dark stone as the road outside, but here there were pavements that stood so high above the road that a man needed to make quite an effort to step up onto them. At regular intervals, massive stone blocks were set into the road with gaps wide enough for cart wheels to pass between them, but high enough that pedestrians could cross without stepping down into the road.

Carbo hoisted Bartolo up onto the pavement and then along a bit until he reached the broken-down wall of some once-magnificent structure. He settled Bartolo on the wall, in deep shadow.

'Now it's time you tell us everything.'

'Would it be too much to ask for a drink before I do?' Bartolo said faintly.

'You use everything at your disposal to delay, don't you?' Carbo said, but he reached into his sling bag and drew out his drinking pouch. It looked close to empty, but Bartolo was able to squeeze out a last few drops of wine.

'Do you promise to take me where I need to go once I have told you everything?'

'I will take you. Brother Galen and Brother Alcuin will stay here. I can't risk their safety any further.'

'My, but you are prudent,' Bartolo said in his cynical tone.

It was all they could use to tell how he was feeling, for night had fallen and Bartolo was sitting in deep shadow.

'What happened to the cult?' Galen asked as he eased himself out of Alcuin's grip and also settled on the wall.

It was close enough to Bartolo that they could hear each other. It was even close enough that if Bartolo wished, he could lean forward and touch Galen, but not easily.

Bartolo sighed and said, 'I suppose I owe you that much.'

'Were you a faithful follower?'

Alcuin noted he was being careful not to say any names lest they were overheard.

'Ah, that is the nub of the question, isn't it?' Bartolo said. 'But you see, I was never a faithful follower.'

'You weren't?'

It surprised Alcuin to hear that. He'd been puzzling over the mystery all day too. He might not be as intensely curious as Galen, but he wanted to know as well.

'I am a monk and loyal to the church and the pope,' Bartolo said.

'Then why were you with the cult?' Galen asked.

'Because they ordered me to join them. Pope Gregory V is a young man and, though it pains me to say it, insecure in his role. He is terrified of what the coming millennium will bring because of all the portents that have come before.

'Earthquakes have rocked Rome, plague has swept through, as well as wave after wave of invasions. It is exactly as the Book of Revelation has predicted. Not only that, but earlier this year, the pope ousted the anti-pope, John XVI, and had to battle the self-proclaimed ruler of Rome, Crescentius II, who installed the anti-pope.

'That was a bloody battle, since Crescentius holed up in the Castel Sant'Angelo - the largest, most impregnable fortress in Rome. He was finally hauled from there and executed. But you can imagine how this whole business upset the pope.

'And just when everything is looking so precarious, cults began springing up. They seem to be more plentiful than the crops our people need so badly.'

'All the same, to erase a cult without even holding a trial...'

'That is because of who Marozia was,' Bartolo said, sinking his voice at her name.

'A Theophylact?'

'Ah, you are well informed. That family, until our present Pope Gregory, held a great deal of power. Having so recently dealt with one uprising, the pope wasn't willing to let a new one fester to the point that it gained widespread popular support.'

'He nipped it in the bud,' Alcuin said.

'As quietly as possible so that it had no hope of upsetting his rule.'

'The pope,' Galen murmured, and Alcuin wished he could see his friend's expressive face to understand what he was thinking.

'But if that was the case, why did you leave the cult? What were you doing in the County of Toulouse?'

'That was at Marozia's request. She sent many of the monks that had joined her out to parley with other cultists. Not just Geoffroi the Heretic, but every single band we heard about. It was like she was sending out diplomatic missions.'

'To have them join her?'

'She needed her followers to be as vast as the ocean to have sufficient influence over the pope. Her family's reputation is such that merely turning up with a few hundred people would not have been sufficient.'

'But she was travelling alone.'

'She underestimated the eccentricity and egos of the other cult leaders. Those we spoke to either wanted to remain in the lands they had fought over or they thought they could do a better job than her and wanted to take over her cult. Others killed her emissaries and, as you know, I got to Geoffroi too late.'

'You and Brother Gentile,' Carbo said.

'Who seemed to be quite willing to speak to you when the two of you were alone,' Alcuin said.

'Ah, so you saw that too.'

Bartolo sounded weaker than he had till now, and it made Alcuin suspect that he and Gentile had been close.

'Gentile and I decided he might make a better spy if he claimed to have taken a vow of silence. People are less careful about what they say around a person who never speaks. He was able to report back on all sorts of conversations, although most were devoted to the cult and had little of interest to say.'

'And what of Marozia? Do you really think she was a threat?' Galen asked.

'It is not for me to question that. The pope ordered me to follow her and report back. That was what I did. Little did I suspect that he would wipe out his servants as well as the cultists.'

'Is that why you stabbed her?' Alcuin said, avoiding saying Marozia's name because of the way Carbo twitched every time Galen did so.

'I thought it would show whose side I was on but, in the end, it made no difference.'

'Now you know everything,' Carbo said in a grumbling tone, a shadow looming over the men sitting on the wall. 'And I shall take this traitor to wherever he needs to go.'

'Why?' Bartolo and Alcuin said in unison.

'Because he clearly no longer has the strength to move on his own, and it will only cause more suspicion if they find his body among these ruins come morning.'

'They will merely take me as another victim of the thieves that terrorise all Rome when night falls,' Bartolo said.

'All the same. I will take you somewhere that you may die and your body be quietly disposed of.'

'And I will respect your discretion and not tell you where that is until we are clear of Brothers Galen and Alcuin. I understand your revulsion of me, Brother Galen,' Bartolo said as Carbo lifted him back onto his feet. 'But you will find that Rome is deeply political. You, too, will be sucked into its maelstrom. If I can do anything to help you, it would be to give you this advice: leave Rome immediately. Don't try to see the pope and don't let anyone know you are a saint. That way you may yet live to see out the year.'

Galen watched as Carbo and Bartolo vanished into the night and his unease grew.

'Do you think he's right?'

Alcuin's grip tightened about his staff, which Galen felt in the hardening of his arm muscle.

'We have come such a long way. We can't just turn around and leave.'

'This place is not what I was expecting.'

'It's more run down and decrepit than I thought it would be too. From the little we saw at sunset, it seems to be more ruins than a functional city.'

'And the politics are even worse than the city,' Galen said and couldn't prevent a shudder.

Alcuin sighed.

'What a day it has been! If it wasn't for the massacre this morning, the two of us would whoop in celebration to have finally arrived in Rome. I mean, Galen, we made it! We travelled all the way from Yarmwick to Rome. We were chased by Vikings and captured by Moors, and yet, here we are. That is quite something, isn't it?'

'I suppose it is.'

Alcuin was right, Galen thought. It was a tremendous achievement. He should have felt victorious. Instead, there was a flatness, a lack of emotion. Perhaps he'd received so many hammer blows to his heart that it was numb.

'It's been such a long time since we left home.'

'But now we're at the end of our journey. We simply have to see the pope, report what we know and then we can leave.'

'The pope,' Galen murmured and wondered what he could ask of a man who'd ordered the obliteration of an entire cult. 'Do you think he would know better than we or Bishop Sigburt what I am?'

'Let's worry about that later. For now, let's just celebrate how far we've come.'

'You're right,' Galen said, thankful that Alcuin was with him. Alcuin, who supported him and cheered him up and who could always be depended upon. 'I'm glad, after all, that you came along.'

'Have there been moments when you regretted it?' Alcuin asked, sounding surprised.

'You have suffered a great deal because you offered to accompany me. Sometimes that fills me with guilt.'

'Well, this time the tables are turned,' Alcuin said with a cheerful laugh. 'For it was I who forced you to come to Rome. So you need no longer feel bad. And after this, I am sure we will get home again. God is on our side.'

'Perhaps He is.'

Galen could no longer doubt that a higher power worked through him at times. Facts built upon undeniable facts. What he made of that was still to be debated. How he would come to a resolution was also unclear, now more than ever. But of one thing he was certain, sitting together in the dark in this unfamiliar city.

'I'm really glad you are my friend,' Galen said, and gave Alcuin's arm a squeeze. 'I believe you are right. Together we can achieve whatever we set our minds to.'

Enjoyed this book?

If you are like me, you use reviews to decide whether you want to buy a book. So if you enjoyed the book, please take a moment to let people know why. The review can be as short as you like.

Thank you very much!

Get all my short stories for FREE!

Building a relationship with my readers is one of the great things about being a writer. That is why I continue to upload a wide collection of short stories for free on my website. These currently include a collection of short stories, and some individual longer short stories including a Galen spin off, a quirky tale about a rabbit in Lisbon and a couple of Christmas romances.

Sign up for my no-spam newsletter that only goes out when there is a new book or freebie available, at: www.marinapacheco.me

ALSO BY

Get all my books here:

MEDIEVAL HISTORICAL FICTION ePub, paperback and hardback

Fraternity of Brothers, *Life of Galen, Book 1* – Cast out for a crime committed against him, his future looks bleak. Until an unexpected visitor gives him hope for justice. A fight for acceptance, absolution and friendship in Anglo-Saxon England.

Comfort of Home, *Life of Galen, Book 2* – Proven innocent, he's returned from exile. Can he recover all that he lost? A tale of friendship and return to a family he thought he'd lost, set in Anglo-Saxon England.

Kindness of Strangers, *Life of Galen, Book 3* – Trapped in a land plagued by vikings, can one small miracle be all they need to survive? A tale of miracles, betrayal and friendship while under viking siege.

The King's Hall, *Life of Galen, Book 4* – As if being commissioned to create a book to turn back the Apocalypse isn't enough, intrigue and romance threaten to destroy

everything he's come to rely upon. Friendship, love and intrigue at the court of King Aethelred the Unready.
Restless Sea, *Life of Galen, Book 5* – Just when they thought they could go home, they're thrust into an adventure at sea. A journey that tests the bonds of friendship.
Friend of My Enemy, *Life of Galen, Book 6* – Captured by an implacable enemy, their future looks bleak. Will escape even be possible?
Road to Rome, *Life of Galen, Book 7* — A journey across a turbulent continent. Will Galen find the answers he seeks?
Eternal City, *Life of Galen, Book 8* — Galen and Alcuin delve into the secrets of the corrupt and decaying city of Medieval Rome.

AUDIOBOOKS narrated by Jacob Daniels
Fraternity of Brothers, *Life of Galen, Book 1*
Comfort of Home, *Life of Galen, Book 2*
Kindness of Strangers, *Life of Galen, Book 3*
The King's Hall, *Life of Galen, Book 4*
Restless Sea, *Life of Galen, Book 5*

HISTORICAL ROMANCE: ePub, paperback, hardback and audiobooks with AI narration
Sanctuary, *a sweet Medieval mystery* – He needs shelter. She wants a way out. Will his brave move to protect risk both their hearts? An optimistic tale of redemption with heart-warming characters and feel-good thrills.
The Duke's Heart, *a sweet Victorian romance* – His body may be weak, but his dreams know no bounds. Will she be the answer to his prayers? A disabled duke, a strong and determined woman and a slow-building relationship.
Duchess in Flight, *a swashbuckling romance* – She's on the run

from a deadly enemy. He lives in the shadows of truth. When their lives merge, will their battle for survival lead to love? A reluctant hero, a woman and her children in distress, a chase to the death.

What the Pauper Did, *a body swap mystery romance* – How do you define yourself? Is it through your appearance, your memories or your soul? Intrigue, murder and romance in an alternate Lisbon of 1770.

CONTEMPORARY ROMANCE ePub, paperback, hardback and audiobooks with AI narration

Scent of Love – Can two polar opposite perfumers overcome their differences and create a unique blend all of their own? Love, intrigue and clashing values in the perfume houses of Lisbon.

Sky Therapy — A detective and the son of a serial killer. Is it safest to stay apart, or will they risk everything for love?

SCIENCE FICTION/ FANTASY ePub and paperback

City of Night, *Eternal City, Book 1* – World-threatening danger, a female demonologist, an unwitting apprentice, a city in a single tower, a satisfying ending.

SHORT STORIES: ePub, paperback, and AI narration

Living, Loving, Longing, Lisbon, Vol 1 & Vol 2 – A collection of short stories inspired by the city of Lisbon, written

by people from around the world who live in, visited or love Lisbon.
Loves of Lisbon – An advent calendar of 24 short, sweet romances of the intertwining lives of the residents of Lisbon.

FREEBIES: ePub and AI narration
Shorties – My shortest works: futuristic, contemporary and historical.
White Rabbit of Lisbon – A whimsical short story. What will happen when a rabbit and a raven fall in love?
Scourge of Demons – How would you deal with your demons? A short story set in the world of the Life of Galen series.
The Greek Gift – A Christmas short story. At the gym he ignored her; will it be any different at the Christmas Eve party?
Christmas Fates – A Christmas short story. Aurora Dawn is about to learn the true meaning of Christmas and it has nothing to do with how many of the latest must-haves she can sell.

ABOUT AUTHOR

Marina Pacheco a binge writer of historical fiction, sweet romance, sci-fi and fantasy novels as well as short stories. She writes easy reading, feel-good novels that are perfect for a commute or to curl up with on a rainy day. She currently lives on the coast just outside Lisbon, after stints in London, Johannesburg, and Bangkok, which all sounds more glamorous than it actually was. Her ambition is to publish 100 books. This is taking considerably longer than she'd anticipated!

You can find out more about Marina Pacheco's work, and download several freebies, on her website: https://marinapacheco.me
Website: https://marinapacheco.me

Sign up to Marina's newsletter via her website or on Substack to keep up to date on all her writing activities, get early previews of covers and first chapters, short stories and freebies.
Follow me on substack:
https://substack.com/@marinapacheco
email: hi@marinapacheco.me

Printed in Great Britain
by Amazon

61741465R00109